W9-AAT-191

DREAMS OF WATER

Nada Awar Jarrar was born in Lebanon to an Australian mother and a Lebanese father. She has lived in London, Paris, Sydney and Washington DC and is currently based in Beirut where she lives with her husband Bassem and their daughter Zeina but, as a result of the outbreak of war in Lebanon, the family was forced to flee to the mountains in search of safety. Nada Awar Jarrar has been vocal in her condemnation of the killing of innocent civilians in this conflict, publishing a piece in *The Times* and contributing to an anthology of writing *Lebanon, Lebanon*, the profits of which went to Save The Children Lebanon. Her first novel, *Somewhere, Home* won the Commonwealth Best First Book award for Southeast Asia and the South Pacific in 2004.

Visit www.AuthorTracker.co.uk for exclusive information on Nada Awar Jarrar.

Praise for *Dreams of Water*:

'This beautifully written book is powerfully evocative of the human cost of war and the longing for love.' *Economist*

'The beauty of this novel lies in its images which are vivid and strange, sometimes even fantastical.' *Times Literary Supplement*

'The characters are surrounded by loss and memory . . . Jarrar presents their stories as fragments, shifting us backwards and forwards in time, stressing the precarious nature of life for those trying to escape physical and emotional distress.' *Metro*

'An absorbing novel which beautifully navigates the themes of love and loss.' *Easy Living Magazine*

'The prizewinning author of *Somewhere, Home*, returns with a moving tale of love, loss, exile and hope, written in lucid, spare prose.' *Sainsbury's Magazine*

'Nada Awar Jarrar's second novel arrives as beautifully and temptingly wrapped as a box of Lebanese sweets.' *Sharq Magazine*

'A moving story about the love, hope and strong ties that bind families.' *First*

'A haunting paean to the confusion of grief, the damage of war, and trauma caused by faith.' *Glasgow Evening Times*

Also by Nada Awar Jarrar

Somewhere, Home

NADA AWAR JARRAR

Dreams of Water

HARPER

This novel is entirely a work of fiction.
The names, characters and incidents portrayed in it are
the work of the author's imagination. Any resemblance to
actual persons, living or dead, events or localities is
entirely coincidental.

Harper
An imprint of HarperCollins*Publishers*
77–85 Fulham Palace Road,
Hammersmith, London W6 8JB

www.harpercollins.co.uk

This paperback edition 2007
1

First published in Great Britain by
HarperCollins*Publishers* 2007

Copyright © Nada Awar Jarrar 2007

Nada Awar Jarrar asserts the moral right to
be identified as the author of this work

A catalogue record for this book is
available from the British Library

ISBN-13: 978-0-00-722196-7

Set in Sabon by Palimpsest Book Production Limited,
Grangemouth, Stirlingshire

Printed and bound in Great Britain by
Clays Ltd, St Ives plc

All rights reserved. No part of this publication may be
reproduced, stored in a retrieval system, or transmitted,
in any form or by any means, electronic, mechanical,
photocopying, recording or otherwise, without the prior
permission of the publishers.

This book is sold subject to the condition that it shall not,
by way of trade or otherwise, be lent, re-sold, hired out or
otherwise circulated without the publisher's prior consent
in any form of binding or cover other than that in which it
is published and without a similar condition including this
condition being imposed on the subsequent purchaser.

*For Aida and Aref and
for Amou Ahmad*

PROLOGUE

S tanding in the back garden of her parents' mountain home, Aneesa, at four, hears the angels, a chorus of sweet voices that tell her to dance for them. She twirls around beds of roses, down a dirt road and into the breeze, humming to herself. When Waddad calls to her, Aneesa stops beneath the shade of a pine tree and takes a deep breath before running indoors.

'Time for lunch,' her mother says. 'Let's wash your hands before you sit down.'

Aneesa stands up on the stool in front of the sink and puts her hands under the tap. Waddad pulls her sleeves up, turns the water on and lathers soap on to her own hands before grabbing Aneesa's and kneading them with cool suds.

'When I call my children in to eat, they wash their hands on their own,' Aneesa says, looking up at Waddad.

'Haven't I told you not to put your dolls in water? You'll ruin them.'

'They are my children, *mama*, not my dolls.'

Waddad wipes Aneesa's hands dry and gently pushes her towards her seat.

'Always talking about children that are not there.' Waddad sounds cross as Aneesa sits down to eat.

Later that day, Waddad takes Aneesa by the hand and they walk down to the village. The sun is strong and wisps of Aneesa's long dark hair stick to her forehead.

'Where are we going, *mama*?'

'We're going to talk to the sheikh,' Waddad replies in a firm tone.

They arrive at a house in a side street just before the main *souq* and go carefully down some stone steps on its side. The door of a basement room is open. An old man sits on the floor, his back propped up by large pillows against the wall behind him, his legs crossed neatly in front of him. He is dressed entirely in dark blue and has a grey-black beard that lies rigid on his chest like a small, coarse broom. He looks intently at Waddad as she speaks. When he opens his mouth to speak, the beard moves up and down with his words.

'The child has spoken of a past life,' he says.

Waddad pushes her hands down on Aneesa's shoulders, the scent of fear emanating from her skin.

'But what am I to do? Her father does not believe in these things and he will be furious if he hears her talking about it again.'

The old man shakes his head so that the white headdress slips forward over his forehead. Then he passes a hand over the length of his face. When he removes it, the stiff beard looks narrower and less impressive.

'She may never speak of it again,' he says.

He shrugs his shoulders and leans forward until his face is very close to Aneesa's. She looks into his bright blue eyes and sniffs at the scent of olive-oil soap coming from his skin. When Aneesa reaches out to touch the beard, she hears her mother gasp and call out her name. She puts her hand down. The sheikh smiles and moves back to rest against the pillows once again.

Father is helping Bassam with his homework. The two of them are sitting at the dining table with books and paper and pencils before them. Aneesa can feel anxiety in the air but is not sure if it is hers or theirs.

'Aneesa,' her father calls out. 'Get me a cup of coffee, will you?'

Aneesa looks up at her father and begins to say something but he stops her.

'Go on, *habibti*,' he says. 'Not too much sugar now.'

Aneesa glances quickly at Bassam and feels her heart sink. He is leaning an elbow on the table and holding his head up with his hand. He looks bored and clearly uninterested in his work. Father will be so angry with him, she thinks. Where has Mother gone?

In the kitchen, Aneesa brings water to the boil in the pot and adds half a teaspoon of sugar, then she puts in the finely ground coffee and stirs gently, taking the pot off the burner just as the mixture begins to come to the boil and then putting it back on again until the coffee is thick and frothy at the edges. She hears her father's raised voice from the dining room.

'Bassam, you're not concentrating. I asked you a

question and I want you to think about the answer before you say anything.'

Bassam murmurs something in reply but she cannot tell what he is saying. Aneesa pours the coffee into a cup.

'What?' Father asks tersely.

Moments later, Aneesa hears her father shout out loud. When she steps into the dining room with the coffee, he is no longer there but Bassam is still in his chair. His head is bent low and he has one hand over his ear. When he looks up at her and removes his hand, Aneesa sees that his face has gone very red. She remains perfectly still as Bassam stands up and slowly walks out of the room.

Aneesa stands on a chair by the kitchen table holding a large loaf of flat bread in her hands. She sees her child self carefully fold the loaf into quarters and then try to put it inside a plastic bag before it unfolds again.

'Are you all right, Aneesa?' Father comes up behind her.

She looks up at him, his round face, bulbous nose and greying hair, and waits for him to smile.

'Shall I help you with that?' he asks.

She nods and watches him hold the folded loaf with one big hand, put it into the bag and then tie the handles of the bag together to make a tight bundle.

'Where are you going with the bread, *habibti*?'

Aneesa steps off the chair.

'I'm taking it to my children. They're hungry.'

He puts his arm around her shoulders and they walk out of the kitchen.

'Take me there, *baba*,' Aneesa pleads. 'I can hear them calling to me. Take me in the car.'

Later that night, as she lies in her bed in the dark, Aneesa hears her parents arguing in the next room. She knows that no matter how loud their voices, they cannot drive away the sound of weeping children that fills her ears.

Waddad spoons a mixture of rice, tomato and parsley on to half-cooked vine leaves that she has placed flat on the kitchen table. Her hair is tied back and her face shines with perspiration. Once each leaf is filled, she rolls it into a small tube and places it in a saucepan. Little Aneesa stands on a chair and peers inside to look at the cigar shapes lined up tightly against one another. She sniffs at the tangy, uncooked smell of the stuffed leaves and feels her mouth water.

'I like the old man best,' Aneesa says.

'What old man, dear?' Waddad's head is bent low and she is not looking at her daughter.

'The one with the beard. I want to see him again.'

'Shhh,' Waddad whispers. 'You know your father doesn't want us to talk of such things.'

'He's out in the garden. He can't hear us.'

'What do you want to see the old man for, anyway?'

Aneesa reaches inside the saucepan, takes out a stuffed vine leaf and pops it into her mouth. The rice makes crunching noises between her teeth as she chews.

'That'll give you stomachache,' Waddad warns.

*   *   *

Bassam follows Father around in the garden carrying a heavy bucket filled with wilted roses. Father examines the bushes closely and expertly snaps off the heads of the flowers at the top of the stem before Bassam rushes to pick them up and put them in the bucket. They are not speaking but Aneesa can tell her brother is itching to be elsewhere. She walks up to them and takes *baba*'s hand.

'Ah, Aneesa,' he says with a gentle voice.

Bassam tries to hand her the bucket.

'Your sister can't carry that, Bassam. It's much too heavy.'

'I'll go and empty this,' Bassam says sulkily. 'It's too full, even for me. I'll be right back.' But Aneesa knows he will not be coming back.

There are times when she imagines she can see her brother in the distance. He is walking down their street, hands in pockets, head bent low. He cannot be more than fifteen years old; his hair is sticking upwards at the crown of his head and in the fragile curve of his long neck, Aneesa sees hints of their childhood. She waves to him but he ignores her. When he finally stops, there are two of him, one standing behind the other, arms wrapped tightly around his twin. They are on a beach in moonlight and she hears them whispering to one another above the sound of waves lapping at their feet.

Somewhere between the village spring and the wilderness, beyond the fragrant fig tree by the grocery shop, Aneesa stands in the single sunny spot in the square. Her eyes are squeezed shut so that blazes of orange line the backs of her eyelids. She raises both arms, palms towards

8

the light, and takes a deep breath. A gentle humming unfolds behind her forehead and her mouth stretches in a smile.

'Aneesa.'

She opens her eyes and turns around. As Waddad approaches through the light and shadow, Aneesa feels a movement in her chest.

'Come on. The sheikh is waiting for us.'

He is sitting outside this time, on a low stool by the front door. His slippers are covered in dust and the front of his baggy navy-blue *sherwal* hangs in folds between his thin legs. A young woman in a black dress and the customary long white *mandeel* brings out two chairs before walking back into the house.

Aneesa shifts forward in her chair so that her feet touch the ground.

The old man lifts a hand to shade his eyes from the sun, puts it down again and looks at her.

'How old are you now?' he asks.

'She's six,' Waddad replies.

The old man grunts loudly and Aneesa leans towards him, placing both hands on her knees.

'Our house was made of stone like this one.' She points to the wall behind the sheikh. 'But it was very small and the ground was uneven. The mattress tilted to one side when we slept and the soles of my children's feet were always black with dirt.'

'What else?' asks the sheikh.

'That's all I remember,' she says, shaking her head.

Waddad shifts in her chair but remains silent.

The sheikh shuffles his old feet and a cloud of dust rises up around them. Aneesa feels suddenly weightless and realizes that she has been holding her breath. When she lets go, the air comes out in a loud sputter. She holds a hand up to her mouth and hangs her head before looking up again a moment later.

The young woman in the veil is leaning over Aneesa with a tray in her hands. Aneesa takes a glass of lemonade and says thank you. The old man and Waddad are quiet. Aneesa sips at her drink and sees time close around the three of them in a kind of circle.

They are in the mountains and Aneesa, Waddad and Bassam are in the garden at the front of the house. It is summer and the pine trees around them and in the valley below give out the sticky scents of sap and strong sunlight. Waddad is sitting on the stone bench in the centre of the garden with a tray in her lap on which there are two bowls; one is filled with raw minced meat mixed with *bulghur* and the other with fried pine nuts and pieces of cooked minced meat for stuffing. Aneesa is standing beside her and Bassam is kicking a football aimlessly on the small patch of lawn around the bench. Aneesa wishes he would either stop or let her join in.

'I want to play too,' she says.

'Stop whining,' Bassam retorts and then kicks the ball past her and into a tree trunk just behind Waddad.

'Bassam,' Waddad says in a warning voice.

'She's always bothering me, *mama*. Make her stop.'

Aneesa lunges after her brother but he slips away and turns around and grins at her. She reaches for the ball, lifts it above her head and aims at him. He moves quickly to one side and the ball misses him.

'Stop it, you two,' Waddad says absently. 'Come and learn how to do this.'

Waddad is making small, stuffed *kibbeh* which she will later fry for lunch. She rolls a handful of raw meat and *bulghur* into a ball with one hand which she pierces with the index finger of the other. Then she fills the hole with the stuffing and closes it up at both ends into two neat points, creating an oval shape that bulges out in the middle.

Bassam sits down beside her and watches carefully.

'I bet I could do that,' he says with a chuckle.

'Your hands are dirty.'

'I mean if my hands were clean.'

Waddad looks up at him and smiles before returning to her work.

'Mmmm,' she murmurs.

Aneesa bends down to pick up the ball and holds it closely to her chest as she watches them. She sniffs loudly and begins to move towards the bench but her mother and brother do not look up at her. She stops and looks at them again, this time more carefully. They are both very intent on the task before them: Bassam, focusing so completely on his mother's hands that he seems to be equally involved in its success, and Waddad, her shoulders slightly hunched up with the delicate effort, revelling in the attention. They are perfect together, she thinks, and is surprised at the clarity in this discovery. She lets go of the ball and feels a shiver go through her body. I am growing up, Aneesa murmurs to herself and lifts her hands to her hips. These are all the things I can see.

PART ONE

The first time Aneesa sees Salah she is waiting at the bus stop near her home. He sits beside her on the plastic perch attached to the bus shelter and immediately the scent of fresh lemon fills her nostrils. His woollen jacket is zipped halfway up so that the denim shirt he is wearing underneath it shows through, and his hair, longish and beautifully white, is brushed back from his forehead.

'Hello,' Aneesa hears herself saying.

'Oh!'

'I startled you,' she continues. 'I'm sorry.'

Salah looks flustered.

'No, not at all. I was just lost in my thoughts for a moment.'

She nods and turns to look at the traffic moving towards them. Moments pass before she speaks again.

'Do you think that if we stare hard enough the bus will finally appear?' Aneesa laughs.

*   *   *

Salah, my dear.

My other life seems far away now that I am back, but not you and not our beautiful adventures together. Those things and you I miss terribly. It's not that I'm having difficulty getting accustomed to life at home – there is something of that, though it does not occupy my thoughts very much – it's the ease with which I have slipped back into being here. Lebanon is like a second skin that does not leave me even as I wish it away. It is the here and now of everything I feel and do.

I imagine you, walking down the busy streets of this city in your long brown suede jacket, and when I go past the block of flats you once lived in, I wish I could run upstairs, ring the bell and find you there. We would make tea biscuits, I think, to remind ourselves of our once-Western lives.

In the back of my mind are thoughts of how we met, both of us in the throes of aloneness, almost content with its settled rhythms, yet feeling the desolation that inevitably comes with it. Is that how we became such fast friends?

Did we not find, Salah, besides the solitude, a relief in each other's company that usually comes with a much longer acquaintance? Our mountain people would say we were only two old souls recognizing one another after a long absence.

Waddad is in the kitchen stirring a pot of Arabic coffee over the stove. The smell is strong and pleasing. Aneesa watches as she lifts the dark, thick liquid with the spoon and lets it fall back into the pot. She bends over her mother and plants a kiss on her cheek.

'Good morning, *mama*.'

'Good morning, *habibti*. Sit down and I'll pour the coffee.'

Waddad's hair curls daintily around her long face and her eyebrows are faint lines above watery grey eyes. She is dressed in dark blue jeans and a white T-shirt and looks like a twelve-year-old boy, clean and sweet-smelling first thing in the morning. Aneesa can hardly believe that this is the middle-aged woman she left behind all those years ago.

The two women sip their coffee noisily and with enjoyment, the scent of cardamom seeds rising from the steaming cups.

'I think I've found your brother,' Waddad says moments later.

'What?'

Waddad stands up and turns away to place her cup in the sink. She turns the tap on and reaches for the washing-up sponge.

'What are you talking about, *mama*?' Aneesa jumps up from her seat. 'Where is he? What's going on?'

'Things changed so much for me after you left,' Waddad continues over the sound of the running water. 'I had to manage the search on my own. It took a long time, but it's finally happened.'

Aneesa walks up to Waddad, places her hands on the older woman's shoulders and gently turns her round so they are facing one another. Soapsuds trickle down on the floor between them.

'Mother, what do you mean? Where have you found him? Why haven't you said anything about this to me before? For heaven's sake, tell me what's going on.'

Waddad smiles and continues as though she has not been interrupted.

'He's at the orphanage in the mountains. I've been going there on a regular basis for a few weeks now. We've become friends.' She wriggles out of Aneesa's grasp and turns to the washing up again. 'His name is Ramzi and he is eight years old. He was born only a few days after your brother disappeared. It all fits in.'

Aneesa does not understand at first, then she realizes exactly what her mother is saying.

'What have you done, *mama*? What have you done?'

Waddad rinses her hands and turns to her daughter once again.

'Aneesa, it's time we accepted the fact that your brother is gone. We have to get on with our lives.'

'But what about the letters we received from him while he was being held captive?'

Waddad lifts a hand to Aneesa's face.

'No more letters, Aneesa. No more. Please.'

As an adolescent, Bassam had not grown very tall and had developed a weedy frame that made him bend slightly forwards when he walked so that he seemed almost defenceless. Aneesa used to walk up to him and poke him in the back to make him straighten up. She remembers the feel of the hollow in his thin back.

'I'll take you to see Ramzi one day if you like,' Waddad continues. 'But you have to promise.'

'Promise what, *mama*?'

There is a pause before she replies.

'Just that you'll see the truth as I do.'

*   *   *

Away from home, Aneesa dreams exhilarating dreams of her brother. They are moving together towards a sense of effortlessness.

'Whenever you're ready, Aneesa,' Bassam finally says after what seems a long time in flight.

She is holding on to his arm and watches as he lifts off pieces of the surrounding landscape and moulds them into a vibrant picture of faces and places they have known together.

'That's beautiful,' she tells him before waking up sweating in her bed.

She saw a psychic after she left home, in the hope that he would tell her something about the truth behind her brother's disappearance.

The man sat in a faded velvet armchair: a thin, arrogant man with long fair hair brushed back off his forehead. Aneesa took an immediate dislike to him.

'You have perhaps a father or brother who was killed?' the man asked soon after she had sat down.

She tried not to look too surprised.

'My brother, in the civil war in Lebanon. He was kidnapped and we never saw him again.'

'He's with us now,' the man continued. 'He wants to let you know that he doesn't regret what he did.'

'He's dead?'

The man said nothing.

'What does he look like?' Aneesa blurted out.

'Is that a trick question?' The man gave a harsh laugh. She shook her head.

'That's not what I meant.'

'I'm sorry,' the man said, lifting his hand to his head. 'He's got a large scar on his forehead. He says they killed him three days after he was taken away.' Then he reached over and placed his hand over hers. 'He wants you to stop worrying about him. Tell your mother too.'

She closed her eyes and sat in silence for the rest of the session, strangely comforted by the unlovable man in the armchair opposite.

Did I ever tell you, Salah, what happened after my father died? We no longer went up to the village in the mountains. I told my mother that I missed the smells there and the slanting sunlight that passed over rocks and gorse bush and ruffled them like the wind. I knew Father's spirit was waiting for me there. He's in the garden, mama, I said, pruning the rose bushes like he used to. I saw him in a dream. This is our only home now, she said, making a sweeping gesture with her arms that encompassed the flat, the streets below, Beirut and perhaps even the sea. You're too old, Aneesa, to make up stories, even if you do miss your father. Forget the mountains and the village. And I did, growing up into never looking back, drifting into a kind of living.

Soon after Bassam's disappearance, I arrived home one day to find my mother sitting on my brother's bed surrounded by papers. She had found them in the back of his cupboard, hundreds of political leaflets and lists of names that she did not recognize. She asked me if I had known anything about them. I told her Bassam had mentioned his political involvement but did not elaborate much. I don't want to put your life in danger as well, Bassam had said to me.

My mother stood up, grasped me by the arms and shook me hard. You never bothered to tell me about it, you silly girl, she said, her voice rising. You never took the trouble to tell me. Then she burst into tears.

There are times when I wish I had told you all this when we were together but I was afraid of spoiling the quiet joy we felt in our friendship, of harming it with unrelenting sadness.

Perhaps there were many things you would have liked to tell me too, Salah, but never did. Whenever we were together we seemed to speak more of everyday things, steering a long way from the vagaries of our troubled minds. I remember sitting on the floor in the drawing room of your house on that very cold night when snow covered the streets of the city, a fire in the huge stone fireplace, talking of Lebanon. I rubbed the palm of my hand on the carpet beneath me and looked down at the blue, beige and soft white images of birds and deer in its weave. I told you there were times when I liked it in this city with its pockets of green, and the loneliness and peace it brought me. Trouble seems such a long way away, I said. When I told you the story of my brother's abduction, you asked if that was why I had left in the first place. I nodded and you paused before saying: I'm glad you came here, Aneesa. I mean, I'm glad I met you.

It is mid-morning and Aneesa and her mother have had another argument about Bassam. It is raining hard outside and Aneesa decides to walk along the Beirut Corniche. Big drops of rain splash heavily on to the uneven pavement and on the crests of the mounting waves. She adjusts the hood of her jacket and digs her hands into her pockets.

There are stone benches at regular intervals, each shaped like a flat, squat S, and at the end of the pavement a blue iron balustrade that is bent and broken in places overlooking the sea. There are also tall palm trees planted in a long line on one side of the pavement with what look like burlap bags covering their underside, high up where the remaining leaves flutter in the wind. And if she turns her head to look across the street, beyond the central reservation where flowery shrubs lie almost flush against the deep, dark earth, she sees a number of high-rise buildings that had not been there before she left.

Along the water's edge, fishermen stand in their plastic slippers on rocks covered in seaweed, their lines rising and falling with the movement of the sea. How many fish do they have to catch to make the effort worthwhile, Aneesa wonders?

A man on crutches walks up to her and stops to extend a box filled with coloured packets of chewing gum. She gives him some money and moves on. The poor have always been here. That is familiar, as is the smell of the sea, a murky, damp smell that is welcome after all the years away.

She reaches the end of the Corniche where the pavement becomes wider and curves around a bend in the road, and stops for a moment to watch as men make their way into a mosque across the street. They pass through a small gate, take their shoes off and enter at the front door to perform the noon prayer. Up ahead, between where she is standing and the buildings diagonally opposite, there is a wide two-way avenue crowded with beeping cars and pedestrians with umbrellas over their heads. Some of the trees planted in the central strip are high enough so that she cannot see through to the other side, but she can hear everything, life and her own heart, humming together.

These are the hours of her undoing, long and sleepless, solitary. She shades her eyes and reaches for the bedside lamp. When she lifts herself off the bed, her body shadowing the dim light, she lets out a sigh and shakes her head. Her dreams, gathering all her fears together in one great deluge until there seems to be no means of overcoming them, were once again of water, the images behind her eyes thick and overwhelming, her pulse quickening and then suddenly stopping in the base of her throat.

She tiptoes into the living room in bare feet, switches on the overhead light and stands still for a moment.

'Aneesa,' Waddad calls out from her bedroom. 'Are you all right?'

'I'm fine, *mama*. Go back to sleep now.'

Her mother coughs into the night.

'Don't stay up too late then, dear.'

Aneesa steps out on to the balcony. Beirut in early autumn: the nights are getting cooler though the air remains humid. She wraps her arms around her body and looks down on to the street where there is absolute quiet. She feels a sudden longing for permanence and certainty, for the hardiness she has seen in large oak trees in the West, unwavering and placid too. For a moment, as a breeze comes in from the sea, she wishes she could fly back with it to anywhere but here.

Months after her return, she is still unused to the feeling of always being in familiar places, indoors and out, as if enveloped in something almost transparent that moves with her, a constant companion. These streets, she thinks when she wanders through them, are a part of me, how familiar are the smells that emanate from them, fragrant and sour, the sun that shines or does not on their pavements, and when the rain falls I, umbrella in hand, mince my way through the water, through the cold.

The first letter arrived not long after Bassam's car was found abandoned and empty in a car park not far from the airport. My mother saw the white envelope addressed to her on the doorstep when she opened the front door to put out the rubbish. She brought the envelope inside, and sat down heavily on her favourite kitchen chair before handing it to me. Open it, she said.

I tore open the envelope with trembling hands, pulled the letter out and began to read.

'My darling mother. I cannot imagine how difficult it has been for you and Aneesa these past few weeks and I am sorry for it.'

I looked up at my mother and she nodded for me to continue.

I have already begun negotiating with my captors for my release. It's a long process, mama, so it might be a while before I see you and my darling sister again. I do not know which part of the country we're in but please don't worry about me. I am well and getting plenty of food. I have even made friends with one of the guards here and he has agreed to take this letter for me. I cannot say

*much more and don't know when I'll be able to write
again. I love you both very much.*

I reached out and placed a hand on my mother's
shoulder. Bassam is alive, mama, I said.

She took the letter from me and put it back into the
envelope. Then she stood up and began to pace across
the kitchen floor.

He may have been alive when he wrote this but how
do we know what's happened to him since? my mother
asked. The only way we'll know that he's still alive is if
we see him again. And with that, she turned abruptly to
the sink and began to wash the breakfast dishes.

When we were children, I used to place my hand on
my brother's forehead as he slept and try to will him to
dream of a stronger, hero-like self, of the man he would
be, until he woke up and pushed my hand away. Aneesa,
what are you doing here in the middle of the night? Let
me sleep now.

That moment in my mother's kitchen, suddenly realizing that Bassam's living and dying, both, were endless,
our fears and hopes entangled between them, I shuddered.

Another letter, I murmured to my mother's back.
Another letter?

They drive south along the coast and then turn up into the
hills east of Beirut. When they are halfway there, Aneesa
stops the car and steps out to look at the view. The sun is
shining, the sea is bright and blue, and the air is so much
cleaner up here that she feels she is breathing freely for the
first time since her return. She gets back into the car and
realizes how much she has missed the mountains.

When they arrive at their destination, Waddad and Aneesa stand at the terrace's edge and look down to the valley, into the distance. There are pine trees and gorse bushes and a soft haze in the air. Behind them are mountains of grey rock and fine, violet-coloured earth.

'Shall we go into the shrine now, *mama*?'

'We'll have to put these on.'

Waddad opens her handbag and takes out two long white veils. Aneesa shakes out a *mandeel*, jerking it up suddenly so that it will not touch the floor. The delicate spun cotton flutters outwards. She places it on her head, throws its folds over one shoulder and takes a deep breath.

'It smells so sweet.' Aneesa smiles at her mother.

Waddad reaches for her daughter's hand and the two women make their way to the shrine. They take off their shoes, placing them neatly outside the door before stepping into the large, square-shaped room.

Several people stand leaning against the iron balustrade around the shrine. Aneesa watches a woman who is kneeling, both her hands wrapped around the railing and her eyes squeezed tightly shut.

'Let's sit over there.' Waddad motions towards quilted cushions placed over the large Persian carpet that covers the floor.

They move to one corner of the room and sit down, their legs tucked beneath them. Waddad places her hands on her thighs, stares straight ahead and begins to mutter softly under her breath. She has a serious look on her face and the edges of the *mandeel* rest open against her large ears. Aneesa tries to suppress a smile and fails.

Some moments later, a man tiptoes into the room in

his socks. He must be taking a break from work, Aneesa thinks, because he is wearing navy trousers and a beige shirt that are dotted with dust and paint. He walks up to the shrine and pushes a folded banknote into the collection box hanging on the railing. He stands still for a moment and taps his roughened hand on the wooden box, while gazing at the shrine. Aneesa wonders what he is praying for and watches as he silently steals back out of the room. The kneeling woman is weeping quietly to herself. Aneesa stretches her legs out and coughs quietly. She feels her mother's hand on her arm.

'Shush, dear. I'm trying to concentrate,' she whispers.

'What on?'

Waddad presses her lips together and shakes her head. Moments later, she stands up.

'Come on, Aneesa,' she says, 'let's go.'

When they are back in the car, their heads bare and shoes on their feet, Aneesa and Waddad sit quietly for a moment.

'I was praying for your brother's soul,' Waddad finally says.

'What good does it do?' Aneesa rolls down her window and lets in a cool breeze that touches their faces. She reaches a hand up to her hair, missing the feel of the veil around her head and on her shoulders.

'What other choice do we have?' Waddad asks.

Salah, when I first returned and would come upon strangers talking on a bus or in the street, I could not tell whether they had just met or had known one another a lifetime. The gestures were always the same, the words

27

delivered up close, voices loud, hands moving wildly, touching shoulders or arms or the tops of dark heads. I could not believe at first how distant I had become in my years in London, how cool compared to the heated passions that I found here. Then there was the open curiosity and warmth in people's eyes; neighbours and acquaintances who looked closely at me until I thought I would burn under their gazes. Who are you now? they seemed to be saying to me. What do you make of us after all this time? And I sometimes wanted to walk up to them, perhaps put a hand on a listening shoulder, and say I was sorry for having left them for so long.

The first time you and I met at the bus stop around the corner from my flat in London, I wanted to tell you my story because there seemed something familiar about you. You were perched next to me under the awning and stared, not rudely but in a curious way, as if you saw something recognizable in me too.

When I spoke, you blushed and lifted a trembling hand to smooth back the white hair on your elegant head.

I told you my name and you said: Aneesa, the kind and friendly one. It seemed understandable then that you spoke Arabic and that we were natural companions. You reached out to shake my hand and told me your name and for a moment, as we held on to each other amidst the crowd, it was as though we were the only two people standing there, on a grey day when sunlight was not a possibility.

They sit on the top deck of the number nine bus headed for a leafy suburb. This is their second trip there and Salah has on his lap a bagful of stale bread.

Salah is in his suede jacket and Aneesa has on a new plaid cloak with slits on either side for her arms to go through.

'I didn't think you'd be willing to come out in this weather,' Salah turns and says.

The windows have misted over from the rain and cold and the bus is moving slowly through the traffic.

Aneesa reaches over and pulls the window open slightly to let the fresh air in.

'What does Samir think of our excursions?' she asks.

Salah looks startled at her question and shrugs his shoulders.

'Doesn't he ever ask you what you do with your time while he's at work?'

'I suppose we don't talk very much, my son and I,' Salah says.

They look out of the window again, down at the rows of semi-detached houses and at the figures on the pavement carrying umbrellas and wrapped up in coats and heavy rainwear. Aneesa pulls her cloak more tightly around herself.

'When I first came here, I'd always ride upstairs on the buses,' she says.

By the time the bus reaches the end of the line, Aneesa and Salah are the only passengers. They make their way down the winding steps, Salah opening his large umbrella once they are in the street. They huddle beneath it and walk briskly towards the park where they stand beneath the empty branches of a large tree by the water, both reaching into the plastic bag at the same time. Aneesa breaks the bread into small pieces, throws them into the pond and watches as noisy ducks and geese move effortlessly into the water towards them. Once Salah and Aneesa have thrown all the bread into the water and the bag is finally empty, the birds turn their backs and pedal furiously towards the other edge of the pond.

'Let's sit on the bench there,' Aneesa says, pointing just beyond the tree.

'It may be wet.' Salah opens up the umbrella again.

'Don't worry, this cloak is waterproof. We'll be fine.'

Salah chuckles, puts the plastic bag on the bench and they sit down on it.

The rain has turned into a fine drizzle and a low fog covers the park, somehow intensifying the quiet. Suddenly, they hear song rising from the other side of the pond. The male voice, strong and tender, expertly meanders in and out of the unfamiliar melody, enveloping them in its beauty. Aneesa cannot make out the words to the song and when she turns to look at Salah, his eyes are opened wide with astonishment. She reaches out to him. They sit, gloved hands held tightly together, their breath floating back into the music and the mist.

'When your father collapsed at work, it was Bassam who told me about it,' Waddad says, looking at Aneesa to make sure she is listening. 'He was only fifteen. He came in carrying heavy shopping bags. I was just pleased at the time that he'd thought to get the groceries.

'While I was emptying the bags in the kitchen, I found a bottle of flower water among the things. I couldn't think why he'd bought it. I'd never known him ask for anything like that.'

Waddad is sitting on Aneesa's bed. She looks down and pulls at her nightgown. It is white and much too large for her small frame.

'He seemed irritated when I asked him about it and said I should know that he liked it in his rice pudding.' Waddad looks up at Aneesa again and blinks. 'He always hated rice pudding, even as a child.'

Aneesa leans against the headboard of her bed, her eyes half-closed with tiredness, and waits for her mother to continue.

'Then I realized later, after Bassam told me about your father, when he poured the flower water on a handkerchief and placed it over my face to revive me, I realized that he'd bought it for me all along.'

My mother's search for Bassam began soon after my departure. It took her to distant corners of the city, through streets where the buildings rested close against one another, and the people moved shoulder to shoulder, jostling for space. She climbed up endless stairways, knocking on doors, sipping cups of coffee and waiting to hear a sign of recognition at her story.

I wish I could help you, friends and strangers said. May Allah give you all the strength you need to endure this great sorrow.

She heard about an organization set up by families of the missing and went to one of their meetings. They sat in a small room in an apartment not far from the city centre. There were many of them, men and women, young and old, all with the same anticipatory look in their eyes, as if their loved one might suddenly appear to hold and reassure them, as if the answer lay in talking to each other, in making words of their loss and weaving the uncertainty into the stories of their lives. When it was my mother's turn to speak, she shook her head and stepped determinedly out of the room muttering under her breath, I am not one of them. This is not my place.

She went to the police station in her area and asked to see the officer in charge. He gave her a cup of unsweetened coffee and listened politely until she finished speaking, then he opened a drawer in his dilapidated old desk and took out a ream of paper. I have here a list of all the people who have gone missing in this war, he said. Their families are all desperate for news, just like you, but all I can do is write names down and put them away again.

It was then, dear Salah, that she noticed how tattered his uniform looked. The grey material was frayed at the edges and the buttons down the front of his jacket did not match.

When she finally decided to go and and see the leader of the community, a politician, at his mountain palace, my mother had not yet given up hope.

He looked younger than she had thought he would and kept shifting restlessly in the seat of his armchair. She confided in him her worst nightmare. I just want to know, Waddad said, I want to know what happened. Even if he's never coming back, I need to know what happened to him.

The man only shook his head and she sensed that he might be getting impatient with her.

You must try to forget him, he declared, leaning forward and putting a hand on her arm. It all happened a long time ago. Why don't you busy yourself with some charity work? If you like children, we're always looking for help at our community centres.

*Once outside, Waddad walked into the palace court-
yard and sat on one of the stone steps that surrounded
it. She listened to the water from the garden fountain
slapping against the marble slabs at its outer edge,
wrapped her cardigan more tightly around her and whis-
tled softly to herself.*

*I imagine that my mother knew then that there
was not much she could do about other people's obsti-
nacy except take it on her own shoulders. Maybe it
was that moment in the palace courtyard when her
anger had suddenly abandoned her and she felt so
bereft that she realized she had been looking in all the wrong
places and suddenly knew exactly what she must do.*

'Are you working, dear?' Waddad asks.

Aneesa is sitting at the dining table with a large
Arabic–English dictionary and the document that she is
attempting to translate before her.

'I can't seem to concentrate on work today,' she says,
looking up at her mother.

Waddad is standing by the sofa, one hand against the
back of it, and is running her fingers through her short
hair with the other. She is dressed in her daily uniform
of jeans and T-shirt.

'Tell me, *mama*. What made you change your look so
drastically?'

Waddad gives a little grunt.

'It's more practical this way. No wasting time over hair-
dressers and dressmakers. Besides, you get used to it eventually.'

Aneesa shakes her head.

'But what possessed you to have your hair cut so short?'
'You don't like it?'

Aneesa looks closely at the elfin face. It is long and tired-looking in places but seems self-contained and there is a certain fire in the eyes that she remembers seeing in Bassam's face sometimes. Aneesa feels a shudder go through her body.

'Yes, I do, *mama*,' she says quietly, returning to her work. 'I like it very much.'

There are days when Aneesa thinks that if she could only concentrate hard enough she could make herself forget for hours at a time that there is a war raging around them. As it is, she can only manage a few moments of peacefulness before her mind interrupts it and she is aware of the presence of violence all around her.

To her mother, and at moments like these, Aneesa speaks harshly and with impatience as if it were up to Waddad to change things, to bring Father back and get them out of the chaos in which they now find themselves.

'At least take us up to the house in the village,' Aneesa shouts at Waddad during a particularly vicious battle between militias a few streets away from their block of flats. 'We'll be safer there.'

The two of them are sitting in the corner of the kitchen away from the main road.

'I'm not leaving Bassam here in Beirut and you know there's no way he would come up to the mountains,' Waddad replies with determination in her voice.

'So we have to put up with this because he's foolish enough to want to stay here?'

Aneesa stands up abruptly and moves her hand away

when Waddad tries to pull her down again. Moments later there is a sudden lull in the fighting and they hear the front door being opened. Waddad stands up from her crouching position as Bassam walks into the kitchen.

'Where have you been?'

'Are you two all right?' Bassam asks them and goes to Waddad. 'Sit down, *mama*, please. The fighting has stopped for now. You too, Aneesa. Sit down.'

Aneesa saw Bassam leaving the house hours before the fighting began while her mother was out getting the groceries. She knows he will not tell them where he really was no matter how persistent Waddad is in her questions. She decides to steer the conversation clear of any potential argument and reaches for her mother's hand.

'I'm sorry for shouting at you,' Aneesa says quietly.

'It's all right, *habibti*. We were both afraid.'

Waddad pats Aneesa's hand but she is looking intently at Bassam. Her brother sits down.

'Everything is going to be fine,' he says. 'We'll be fine.'

He puts a hand on Aneesa's hair and smooths it back, then he sits back in his chair and sighs.

A rush of wind follows him when he steps outside and Aneesa closes her eyes as he walks past. The front door slams firmly after him and she is left with an impression of a pair of startled eyes and a sense of anxiety. She takes a deep breath.

Salah is standing beside her. His hand on her arm, he leads her inside. They walk slowly through the large house with windows long as doors and elaborate colour schemes in every room.

'Was that Samir?' she finally asks.

Salah nods.

'I didn't get a chance to introduce you,' he says. 'He couldn't stay.'

They sit on stools at an island in the middle of a kitchen painted in warm yellow. The colour makes Aneesa think of sunlight beaming through half-open doorways. A beautiful floral tea set is laid out on the counter. Salah pushes a plate filled with neatly cut squares of semolina cake towards her.

'Thank you,' Aneesa says, taking a piece of the cake and biting into it. 'This is his house, isn't it?'

Salah begins to pour the tea.

'My son brought me here from Beirut after his mother's death. He said he didn't want me to be on my own.' He passes Aneesa a cup of tea. 'You don't take sugar, do you?' Salah asks.

Aneesa shakes her head and sips at the hot tea. It is strong and satisfying.

'Maybe I'll meet him next time I come,' she says.

'Sometimes, you know,' Salah continues, 'I think he's lonelier than I am.'

She wakes to dreaming, images, faint and gleaming, trailing before her, the colours of her childhood, shades of blues and greens and the warm, nascent yellows of hope. And as she closes her eyes once again, attempting to recapture the clarity of this sudden awareness, of the long journey into the self, she sees herself again and again in the company of those she has loved.

The places they find themselves in are always familiar and magnificent: a sprawling Mediterranean villa in the sun; an old stone house surrounded by tall trees; or a grand home spread over dark red earth, dusty, mysterious and wonderful. The sensation that accompanies the dreams is the same every time: a kind of halting, surprised happiness that threatens to overwhelm her so that she turns to describe it to someone but finds herself suddenly alone.

She wakes up bewildered, wondering where it is all coming from and it is only when she turns on the light by her bed and she realizes she is once again in Beirut that the ghosts of daylight return.

My mother became certain she would find Bassam at the orphanage in the mountains. During her first visit, she asked the directress if she could do volunteer work with the children. After that, she went there twice a week in the afternoons and either supervised the younger ones in the playroom or helped the elementary school children during their study hour. She especially enjoyed the time in the playroom with the younger ones and brought along new toys from time to time. She spent many hours with the children on the floor playing with the farm animals or building high towers with multi-coloured bricks. Sometimes she had a particular project organized and asked all the children to participate in it. They did cardboard cut-outs of a mountain village, complete with houses, trees and prickly bushes, and used some of the animals they already had, placing them among the buildings and stones.

Whenever she helped during study hour, Waddad had to remember to keep her eye out for the boy she wanted to find, always feeling that he was there ready to be discovered. Once or twice, she attended classes where the

37

children were about the right age but nothing came of it. But she continued to look forward to her days at the orphanage, the bus drive up the mountain and back, and the hearts and minds of the little children that she found so compelling. And while she never forgot why she was really there, the urgency of her search had been quelled somewhat so that she was able to hide the visits from me until the day she found him.

Salah, as I write this, my mother sleeps with a happiness I dare not dispel with my doubts. How, I imagine you saying, do you expect me to believe the inventions of a woman torn by grief? How should I read between the words of this story? How can I see, in the birth of an eight-year-old boy, the soul of a man killed at that very moment, moving from one body to another, skin to new skin, time suspended in that movement, transmigration, layers of memory embedded in a young heart and love transported too, as if by magic, burning, passionate and never-ending?

Aneesa decides to buy Salah a pair of gloves for his birthday, something to go with the suede jacket Samir bought him and which he seems to love so much. She goes to a department store in town and finds a pair in tan leather that she knows would look good against the light brown of the jacket. The shop assistant wraps the gloves in two sheets of white tissue paper before placing them in a bag.

When Aneesa hands Salah the gift as they stand waiting for the bus, he looks surprised.

'I know your birthday isn't for a few days yet, but I couldn't wait,' she says.

Salah clings to the bag and looks away, in the direction of the traffic.

'Don't you want to know what it is?'

He opens the bag and pulls out the tissue paper. Looking down at his hands as he attempts to undo the package, trembling, delicate hands with long, tapered fingers, Aneesa feels a rush of tenderness. She takes the parcel from Salah and helps him put the gloves on.

'Do you like them?'

'They're beautiful. Thank you.'

'They're lined on the inside so your hands will stay warm.'

He puts his hands together, interlacing his fingers, and smiles.

Once on the upper deck of the bus, Salah takes off the gloves and places them on his lap, giving them a gentle pat.

'They're very soft,' he says.

The bus lurches forward. Then they both look straight ahead, through the window and towards their approaching destination.

The first time my mother saw him, Ramzi was bouncing a ball in the orphanage playground. It was a cold day in winter and there were other children standing in a loose circle around him. She was overcome with a strong sense of recognition as she watched him toss his head back and smile at his audience. Waddad saw him glance at her and then turn away again. When she approached, she noticed tiny beads of sweat on his forehead where his black hair stuck in wet strips. He had brown eyes and fair skin and was only slightly shorter than she was.

She asked him his name and then told him hers. Are you a teacher? Ramzi asked, the ball hugged tightly to his chest. No, she replied. Ramzi looked shyly up at her, and Waddad heard the children behind her giggle.

Maybe it was his hair, the way it fell in a swirl from the top of his head and over his ears and forehead. He was also the right shape, small and intense, as though every part of his body radiated a singular energy. But most of all, it was the way he looked at her with easy recognition, his mouth breaking into a wide half-grin, half-grimace that had been so characteristic of her own son.

She was beginning to like his name too. Ramzi. She said it out loud to herself at night and felt sure she could become accustomed to it. She was equally certain of her growing affection for the boy, for his disarming, hesitant manner.

When Waddad asked the directress of the orphanage about him, she was told he had been brought in by his mother very recently, a woman with several children whose husband had abandoned her and who had been left to care for them on her own.

Talking with Ramzi on her regular visits, Waddad thought she recognized bewilderment at what had happened to him in his manner, but he was too proud to speak of it to her. Once they were closer, when he trusted her more, Waddad decided she would tell him of their story, of the starry meeting of their souls.

I am aghast, Salah, at my mother's easy fall into dreaming. I had thought her stronger than this, but perhaps

I did not realize the magnitude of her grief. I miss you, our conversations and comforting silences. I miss the slant of tree branches heavy with leaves above our heads as we walked, and the empty air, not quite expectant, but quietly stirring because it was ours alone.

Yours, Aneesa

'He had a girlfriend once, you know,' Salah explains. 'They lived here together for about a year.' He hands Aneesa a wooden spoon and tells her to stir the brown mixture on the stove slowly. 'Don't stop, otherwise it will stick to the bottom of the pan.'

Aneesa stirs the powdered rice and water again and again and sniffs at the fragrant spices that waft up towards her.

'Cinnamon and cardamom, right?' she calls to Salah as he disappears into the larder. They are in the kitchen making *mughli*. Salah brings out almonds and walnuts which he then soaks in warm water in separate bowls.

'We'll need shredded coconut as well once the *mughli* has set,' he says.

'How long will it take?'

'Oh, it should be ready in a couple of hours for after dinner.'

Aneesa is reminded of the times she spent watching her mother preparing meals as a child.

'So it didn't work out?' she asks.

'Sorry?'

'Samir and his friend.'

Salah shakes his head.

'He phoned us one day and said she had left. We never found out what happened.'

41

Aneesa lifts the spoon out of the pot and stares down at the mixture. She wonders what Samir's girlfriend looked like but is too embarrassed to ask.

'Keep stirring.'

'My mother tried very hard to teach me how to cook,' Aneesa says.

'I only started doing it after Huda died, and now Samir enjoys having a hot meal when he gets home from work.'

She pushes her lips tightly together before asking Salah a question.

'Are you happy living here with him?'

Salah stops what he is doing and looks at her.

'I suppose we need each other so much more now,' he says, shrugging his shoulders. He puts a hand into one of the bowls, takes out a handful of almonds and begins to peel them. He has folded his shirt cuffs back so that Aneesa can see his thin forearms and the blue veins on the inside of his wrists.

'I wonder what my mother is doing now,' she says.

'Will he be up there?' Aneesa asks her mother.

'Who?'

'Will the boy be at the orphanage tomorrow?'

'Yes, yes,' replies Waddad, her voice slightly breathless. 'It's a school day. Ramzi will be there. I suppose we should aim to get there around lunchtime.' She reaches up, pulls Aneesa down to her and plants a kiss on her cheek. 'I'll call and let them know we're coming.'

Once at the orphanage, the two women walk through the main building and into a small courtyard. Young trees and rose bushes are planted at regular intervals throughout the garden and a white plastic table and chairs stand under a trellis covered with a wilting vine in one part of the courtyard. They walk on a stone pathway that leads to another section of the old building and through an arched doorway on to an open terrace that overlooks the village.

'We'll wait here for him,' says Waddad.

Ramzi comes out to meet them dressed in a new pair of denims and a blue shirt. His hair is slicked back off his forehead and his face looks like it has been scrubbed very hard.

'This is my daughter Aneesa,' Waddad says.

Ramzi nods and Aneesa takes his hand.

'Hello, Ramzi.'

They stand in an awkward silence before Waddad hustles them away.

'Come on, *habibi*,' she says, putting an arm around the boy. 'Let's show Aneesa around. It's her first visit here.'

He reminds her so much of Bassam as a boy that Aneesa is taken aback. His colouring, the fine down at the top of his hairline, his small frame and the energy that appears stored within it, all of these remind her of her brother. She wants to hold him for a moment, to gather him together, the pieces that have been missing for so long and which she has so badly missed. Instead, she follows him around the orphanage, virtually speechless while her mother chatters in the background, wondering if she will ever again with her mind's eye see Bassam as he had really been.

On one of their excursions, Salah and Aneesa venture down to the river where the city becomes a series of bridges that hang over the dark, muddy water that runs beneath it. They get off the bus and walk at a leisurely pace along the banks of the river, stopping occasionally to look down into it or to sit on the wooden benches placed at even intervals along the pavement. It is a work day and except for a few tourists out sightseeing, there are very few people around them.

This is where London appears truly magnificent, Aneesa thinks. Everything – the roads and bridges and the old buildings, some grimy still and others almost pristine – seems large and beyond her reach. There are no intimate corners here in which one can hide; the river, deep and real and redolent of so much history, is very nearly over-whelming. She feels immeasurably small in its presence.

She takes Salah's arm and stops to look at the scene before them.

'Wonderful, isn't it?' Salah says. 'I never tire of coming here. It reminds me of how unimportant my own concerns can sometimes be.'

'It's a little frightening, though,' she says.

Salah shakes his head and moves closer to the ledge to look out on to the water.

'See how fast it moves?' he asks. 'No single drop of water flows over the same place twice.'

Yes, Aneesa thinks, but it must be very cold and dirty; moving towards everywhere but here. She shudders.

'So, what are you so afraid of, Aneesa?'

They move on, Aneesa letting go of Salah's arm to wrap her scarf more tightly around her neck.

'You know, *habibti*, sometimes I think these are the very things that give me comfort,' Salah says, gesturing at the places and people around them. 'The thought that everything will continue to change no matter how hard

I try to stop it from doing so. That I will grow steadily older, though different and better defined, and that because of this there will always be newness in me too.' He pauses. 'Coming to this city has made me understand many things that I had not been aware of before. It's made me think of myself in a different way.'

Aneesa nods.

'That's happened to me too. But what about all the things we left behind when we left home?'

'They're still here.' Salah taps at his chest. 'I see them in a different light now.' He stops and looks at her. 'You must feel the same way too?'

'I can't forget everything that's happened,' she replies. 'Bassam, my father and what's happened to our country. I can never put those things behind me.'

'That's not what I meant,' Salah says, shaking his head. 'It's not a question of forgetting.'

'What is it then, Salah? What do you think I am meant to do?'

He runs a trembling hand over his hair and smiles.

'Just be happy, my dear. Do just that.'

There is something beautiful about the neighbourhood in winter, Aneesa thinks as she treads carefully through the rain-soaked streets of her childhood, cars splashing through water that streams past gutters, dark, murky, and often smelly. There is something apologetic about it too, long-ago haunts that speak to her in melancholy whispers, and a muffled tenderness in the way the wind strokes her face.

She tries, as she walks, to hold on to her solitude, to feel unfettered again, but there is too much belonging here after all, blatant and unforgiving, reminders of the person she has always been, of the ties that go far beyond what she knows for certain, and into an unsuspecting future.

Today, Bassam and her father are foremost in Aneesa's thoughts. They are part of a general unease that will not leave her, though she tries callously to shake them off, images of their faces, dear and familiar, like lights within her recalcitrant mind. Aneesa, Bassam calls to her as she goes past their once favourite bookshop, do you remember it? *Habibti*, says Father, his voice filled with gentleness, hold on to my hand as we cross the street, that's a good girl now.

In a car park round the corner from her block of flats, she stops to watch children at play. Some are kicking a football about, others have set up a makeshift ramp to fly off with their bicycles and skateboards. A young boy she has seen here before is sitting on the bonnet of an expensive-looking car. He is watching his playmates intently, stillness amidst a sea of movement. For a moment, Aneesa thinks that were she to reach out across the road, through the car park and to that car in the corner, she could touch the boy on his shoulder and he would turn at last to look at her.

Making her way home again, Aneesa remembers what her mother said to her only last night.

'You talk to yourself. I hear you late at night when you cannot sleep and again in the mornings as you move around the house. It is a sign of an unsettled mind, my darling.'

We live and falter, Aneesa decides, in recollection and regret, in the throes of endlessness and the reluctant grace of muted goodbyes. I am hopeless at all of this, at making things work, she says out loud to the indifferent gods and to her fragile, wavering self.

*   *   *

46

The bar is small and filled with smoke and people. Aneesa follows behind Bassam as he pushes his way through the crowd to a counter at the far end of the room by a large glass door. Outside are the darkened shop windows of the small shopping mall in which the bar is located.

'This is Chris,' Bassam says in English, pushing Aneesa towards a man who is sitting at the counter with a glass in his hand.

The man nods at Aneesa.

'What can I get you?' Bassam asks his friend.

'I'm fine, thanks,' Chris says.

He has dark, coarse hair and pale skin and is wearing round wire-rimmed glasses.

'I'll get us something to drink,' Bassam says and moves to the bar.

Someone jostles Aneesa to one side so that she has to reach out and steady herself against the edge of the counter.

'You must be Bassam's little sister,' Chris says.

He looks bored and indifferent and Aneesa decides she does not like him. She straightens herself up and looks round for Bassam but does not find him.

'Don't worry, I won't bite.'

'I didn't think you would,' Aneesa says quickly and regrets the apologetic tone in her voice.

'I'm just kidding,' Chris says with a sudden smile.

Aneesa moves closer to him and leans against the counter.

'What are you doing in Beirut?'

'I'm a journalist.'

Aneesa has never been abroad and this man suddenly seems very exotic to her.

'Bassam has never spoken about you before,' she says.

'Oh? We only met recently. He's helping me with a piece I'm writing about the war for the newspaper I work for.'

'But what does Bassam have to do with the war?'

Chris clears his throat and looks at her more closely.

'Hasn't your brother told you what he's been up to lately?' he asks with a nervous laugh.

Bassam returns with a soft drink for Aneesa and two bottles of beer.

'Pepsi?' He grins at her.

He looks just as he did when he was a young boy, his hair mussed up a little and his shoulders hunched slightly forward. Aneesa feels a rush of tenderness for her brother and turns to frown at Chris.

'What's going on, Chris?' Bassam looks from one to the other. 'What have you been saying to upset my sister?'

'Nothing. It's just uncomfortably crowded in here for me,' Aneesa reaches for her drink. 'Pepsi, no ice, right?'

This is how I imagine it happened, Salah. Ramzi and Waddad sit at one of the large tables by the window in the orphanage dining room. It is early evening and the mist is rising from the valley, moving up through the pine trees and wrapping itself around the building. The damp is palpable.

Are you warm enough? Waddad asks.

Ramzi pulls at the sleeves of the new jumper she has given him and smiles.

They have been sitting there for some time after finishing their meal. It is a few weeks into their relationship and Waddad thinks this is a good opportunity to tell the boy

*about Bassam. She pats Ramzi's arm, leans closer to him
and begins.*

They came to the apartment on a winter morning. There
was a loud banging at the door and someone called out
Bassam's name. When I opened it, a group of men pushed
their way into the hall and asked for him.

*Ramzi nods his dark head and then holds it perfectly
still, as if anxious to hear the rest.*

He used to wake up looking astonished, as if he never
expected to feel so alive first thing in the morning. That
always made me feel good, that look of surprise on his
face, she says.

Ramzi fidgets in his chair and she hurries on.

As they led him away, one of the men told me he
would be back in a couple of hours, that there was just
a small matter that needed to be cleared up. They even
let him go back to his room and get changed before-
hand.

I keep thinking, though . . . I keep wondering why,
when Bassam saw them and realized what was happening,
why he didn't escape through the bedroom window. It
would have been so easy to slip down to the neighbours
and run.

*She lifts her head and looks around the room. The
other children are being unusually quiet over their meal.*

I suppose . . . Ramzi begins.

*Waddad feels her body tense up. Ramzi's eyes wander
and for a moment she thinks he will not continue.*

I suppose Bassam was concerned about you, he finally
says, his voice rising as he speaks.

*Waddad suddenly understands what he is trying to
say.*

Worried they might hurt me? she asks the little boy in the seat beside her. That's why you didn't try to escape, isn't it?

It is a few moments before Waddad allows herself to weep and even then, even as the tears fall down her face and on to her limp hands lying palms up on the table before her, she does not make a sound.

Don't cry, Ramzi pleads. Please don't cry.

The second time Aneesa goes up to the orphanage, she is on her own. She asks for Ramzi and is told by the porter that the children are still in their classrooms.

'I'll just wait over there,' she says, gesturing to the inner courtyard.

'I'll let his teacher know you're here.'

She walks over to the plastic table by the young pine trees, wipes the dust off one of the chairs with the sleeve of her jumper and sits down with her legs outstretched. The vine on the trellis above is mostly brown and dry, but Aneesa notices small green shoots here and there. She looks up, squinting in the thin ray of sunlight that penetrates the courtyard and makes shadows of the wiry vine and of the tree branches.

Moments later, the children emerge from their classrooms yelling in unison. Aneesa looks around and sees Ramzi coming towards her, a ball under his arm. She moves an empty chair nearer to her own and he sits down. For a moment, they are entirely engulfed by the noise around them, and can say nothing to each other. Ramzi's head is bent down and he is holding the ball close to his chest. His trainers, Aneesa notices, are white and very new. Another present from Waddad. She hears Ramzi take a deep breath.

'Would you like to come and watch me play?' he asks her. 'I'm very good.' Then he looks up and smiles at her for the first time.

It is mid-afternoon and Aneesa and Samir are alone together for the first time. They sit in a coffee shop on one side of a long wooden bench, elbows almost touching. Aneesa hangs her head and looks down at her hands encircling a large mug of coffee.

'Thanks for agreeing to meet me here,' Samir begins. 'I wanted to talk to you about my father.'

She looks up at him.

'Salah?'

'He seems to value your friendship a great deal.'

'I know.'

Samir clears his throat.

'You know I brought him away from Beirut just after my mother passed away. Too many memories there for him.'

'You grew up there too, didn't you?'

'I left a long time ago. This is where I live now.'

Aneesa nods. She is beginning to lose interest in the conversation.

'Do you think my father is happy here?' Samir continues.

'Wouldn't it be better if you asked him that yourself?'

He looks slightly flustered.

'I just thought you might have discussed it with him,' he says. 'You seem so close.'

'We are. He is my best friend here.'

Samir lets out a harsh laugh.

'A young woman like you? Surely you have plenty of friends of your own generation.'

She shrugs and takes a gulp of the hot coffee. Then she turns her face away, and gazes through the glass shopfront to the busy street beyond.

'He seems to be growing more and more attached to you. Are you aware of that?'

'But I feel the same way about him.'

Samir shakes his head.

'He is an old man, Aneesa. My father is an old man and he has been through so much. He's very vulnerable and I don't want him hurt. Anyway, I'm not sure you really know him.'

She looks intently at Samir and waits for him to continue.

'Maybe I don't know him too well any more, either. He seems very different from when I was a child. Something has changed and I cannot work out quite what it is. Do you find that strange?'

Aneesa shakes her head.

'You're looking at him with different eyes, I suppose,' she says gently.

Samir smiles and his face is suddenly smooth and bright.

'The first time I went back home I visited the old hotel in the mountains that my parents took me to every summer. In the late afternoons, just before dusk, they would come downstairs after their nap to sit on the terrace. It was spacious and cobblestoned and there were large clay pots filled with geraniums between the tables. We'd sip on lemonade for a few minutes and I would clamber down from my chair and walk over to the edge of the terrace to look out at the world.'

He turns away so she can only see his profile.

'But things had changed,' he continues, shaking his head a little. 'It wasn't so much the building itself, but the exterior grounds. They had installed a canopy in white and yellow stripes with curtains that opened out on to the view. At first, I couldn't quite work out what was wrong, until I realized, looking out at the setting sun, a brilliant haze of red spreading slowly over the sky, that there was a line of young pine trees in view, just below the edge of the terrace.' He looks at her again. 'I was very upset,' he laughs. 'Someone had taken the trouble to plant much-needed trees on the side of the mountain and I was angry because it made everything look different.'

Aneesa sees a small boy in a short-sleeved shirt tucked into starched white trousers. He stands alone, his dark hair combed back off his anxious face, and behind him, a man and woman are silent and waiting too.

She reaches up to place a hand on Samir's arm but he has already shaken off the memory.

'I'll have to get back to the office now,' he says.

Aneesa draws her hand away and places it in her lap. Samir stands up abruptly so that the remaining coffee in his mug spills over on to the counter. She covers his hand with her own as he tries to reach for a napkin.

'Don't worry. I'll clean it up. You go on, I'm going to sit here for a bit and finish my coffee.'

She clutches a handful of paper napkins to her chest and watches as he walks away.

Let me tell you about the boy who would be my brother, Salah.

Ramzi sleeps on the bed closest to the window, where the sunlight comes through to wake him and, in spring, the scent of wildflowers. His clothes go into one half of a cupboard placed between his bed and the bed of the next boy down. The warm jacket Waddad bought him hangs neatly next to the two pairs of trousers he brought with him from home and his new trainers and best shoes are directly underneath on the cupboard floor. Shirts and sweaters go on a shelf and his socks and underwear are in the upper drawer.

He does not mind sharing the cupboard because it is the first time he has ever had a proper place to put his things in. But his own bed is what he enjoys most about being here: sleeping without younger brothers pulling at the covers or kicking him in the shins so that he was always waking up; and sitting cross-legged on the bed during the day, the covers pulled tight beneath him, his shoes off and his books spread across its smooth surface, a fluffy pillow behind him against which to rest his back.

The only time his mother has come to visit since she first brought him here, Ramzi showed her around the dormitory, pointing to his made-up bed and the neatly arranged clothes in the cupboard, and waited for her praise. But she only nodded and looked distractedly around her.

I wish they'd agreed to take one of your brothers as well, she said, shaking her head. They're uncontrollable now that both you and your father are gone.

Ramzi has felt afraid ever since that she would be back with a younger brother for him to take care of, or that she might even decide to take Ramzi away with her to be the man of the house again, just as he had been when

Father left home. But it's not fear that puts him on his best behaviour; Ramzi knows that these things, eating and sleeping well, school and other children and the sojourns in the orphanage playground, all these are the closest he'll ever get to an ordered life, and that is all he wants.

Salah, Salah, what my mother does not know is that I came back not to find Bassam but myself.

Salah is at the door with a large package under one arm. It is his first visit to Aneesa's flat.

'Come in,' Aneesa says. 'Come in. I'm sorry everything is such a mess.'

She has been packing and behind her he can see clothes and objects all over the floor and covering all available surfaces.

He steps inside and, before taking off his coat, hands her the package.

'What is this?'

'It's for you to take home with you.'

She tears off the brown paper and stares at the painting.

'This is the one you brought with you from Beirut, isn't it?'

He nods.

'I can't take it from you, Salah.'

The painting has a narrow gilt frame. Beneath the glass, a wedge of beige cardboard in a rectangular shape surrounds a dark but indistinct figure whose edges trickle into the colours beyond it in bold upwards strokes of yellow, white and light brown. Through the blurriness of it, in the undetermined shapes that surround the figure in the painting, Aneesa sees a circle of wings: two, three or four, she cannot be sure, but feathery and marvellous nonetheless. She touches the angel through the glass with the tips of her fingers.

Salah reaches for her hand.

'It would really make me happy if you took this with you, Aneesa. Please.'

'I'll think of you every time I look at it,' she finally says. She puts the painting down and takes his coat.

The windows are grimy and grey and the plaid coat she's worn so often on their outings together is thrown on the floor in one corner of the room. Salah bends down, picks it up and looks at it for a moment before laying it neatly against the back of a chair. He looks up at Aneesa.

'I shall miss you, my dear,' he says quietly. 'It won't be the same without you here.'

Aneesa begins to cry.

The bird clings to its perch. It is nervous and its feathers, green and white, are ruffled so that its head has sunk deep into its chest. Aneesa lifts the cage gently off the passenger seat next to her to look inside and then puts it down again. The car suddenly lurches forward. The bird begins to fly from one end of the cage to the other, hitting its body against the bars.

'Shush, little darling,' Aneesa calls out in a singing voice. 'We'll soon be there. Settle down now.'

She looks at the bird and thinks for a moment that she can see its heart beating in its little chest. Whatever possessed me to do this? she wonders. She remembers her parents giving her and Bassam a pair of green parakeets when they were very young. Neither of the birds had survived very long. This one is blue. Hopefully it will fare better.

At the orphanage, Aneesa makes her way to the main office and asks to see the directress. She is shown into a bizarrely furnished oblong room with long French windows on one side and a row of green velvet sofas on the other. She places the cage on the floor.

'Welcome.' A short woman with a bouffant hairstyle and high heels walks into the room and shakes Aneesa's hand. 'Please sit down.' The woman glances at the cage and then turns her attention back to Aneesa. 'Your mother is doing wonderful work here, you know,' she says.

'She gets a great deal of satisfaction from being with the children and I am grateful to you for that,' Aneesa says.

The directress's teeth protrude slightly so that when she smiles, her closed lips stretch outwards as well as to either side of her small face, and her eyes, which are small and brown, narrow into slits. Aneesa feels a sudden affection for the woman.

'You know, of course, that my mother has taken a special interest in young Ramzi?'

The directress nods but says nothing.

'It doesn't concern you unduly?' Aneesa continues. 'He already has a family of his own, doesn't he?'

The directress does not reply immediately.

'How do you like your coffee?' she asks Aneesa.

'I'm fine, thank you.'

'The fact is, Ramzi's family can't take care of him right now,' the directress says. She lifts a hand to the collar of her dress before continuing. 'Besides, what's wrong with your mother and that child taking comfort in one another's company?'

Aneesa hears the hushed sound of the flutter of wings coming from the cage beside her.

'But it's just not true,' she protests. 'What she thinks is simply not true.'

The directress stands up and points to the cage.

'Is that for Ramzi?' she asks.

Aneesa looks down at the bird. It has moved to the middle of its perch and is looking around with quick, jerking movements of its head. She nods.

I understand Ramzi better now, Salah. He knows he is not alone in this world but there are times when he is suddenly aware of just how long he has been living at the orphanage, sleeping in his narrow bed by the window, the bird in his cage on the ledge, the breathing of other boys so close that he waits to synchronize it with his own, into a rhythm that finally puts him to sleep.

His mother's visits are infrequent. She has gone away across the border, to the mountain of the Druze where her family is from and has promised Ramzi she will come back for him one day soon. But he has long stopped standing nonchalantly by the orphanage gate on Sundays, waving the other children goodbye and pretending he was waiting for no one. Instead, he spends his day taking care of the bird or exploring the woods that surround the orphanage, stealing away for an hour or two into a copse of trees to lie on his back in the dirt, pine needles pricking him through his clothes, and to watch the movement of blue and grey sky between the branches.

When the idea comes to him, Ramzi is sitting at break-fast early in the morning. The dining room is full and noisy, just as he likes it, and he is eating fried eggs and dipping his bread into a mixture of dried thyme, sesame seeds and olive oil. Just as he breaks off a piece of the thin mountain bread, folding it carefully into a cone-like shape to scoop up a piece of egg, Ramzi realizes what he must do. He eats quickly, sneaks out of the dining room and makes his way to the main office. It is too early for the directress to be there, so he asks the secretary if he can make an urgent telephone call. He slips her a piece of paper and she dials the number for him. Ramzi turns his back to the young woman at the desk as he listens to the ring tone. He puts a hand on his heart and feels it beating very fast.

'Who is that?' he asks.

'Ramzi, it's me, Aneesa. Is everything all right?'

'I want to speak to Waddad.'

I hear disappointment in his voice.

'Can't you tell me about it, Ramzi? Maybe I can help.'

'I . . . I just wanted to let her know that I've made my decision.'

'What decision?'

He clears his throat and I tighten my hand around the receiver.

'Just tell her that I will come and live with her. There's no need to wait any longer. I will come and be her son.'

After all the boxes have been packed and sent away, Aneesa takes her only suitcase out of the cupboard in the hallway and places it on her bed. Inside, there are a couple of empty plastic bags and a small padlock with its keys attached to it. She takes the things out and turns to her wardrobe, pulling out dresses, trousers and tops, thick jumpers, scarves, shoes and jackets and packing them away until the only things left hanging are the things she will wear on her flight back home. She zips up the suitcase, ties a luggage belt around it and fits the padlock into the two holes at each end of the zip. When she pulls the padlock shut, it makes a tiny clicking sound. She straightens up and takes a deep breath.

Later that day, sitting in the armchair in the living room with one leg bent underneath her, Aneesa takes a writing pad and pen and begins to write.

My darling mother and sister,

I hope you haven't been unduly worried. It's been months since I was last able to write. I've been moved, along with the other prisoners, and again I'm not quite certain where I am. I only know that we are too far away to make our way home. They have put me to work in the fields. I enjoy being outdoors for much of the day, and sometimes even manage to forget that I have lost my freedom. I hope that you are both well, that you are also happy in your lives. I am certain that you have taken good care of each other over the years. This thought has been a great comfort to me. I love you both very much and pray that we will one day find one another again.

Bassam

Aneesa lifts the pen off the page and rereads what she has written. The letter is shorter than the previous ones she has written and does not really sound like Bassam. She wipes a tear from her cheek, folds the paper and places it inside a white envelope. Then she puts on her cloak and goes out.

Now that spring is here, Aneesa and Waddad have their morning coffee on the narrow balcony outside the sitting room. There are four chairs around an old table that once belonged in the kitchen of their mountain home. They sit in their dressing gowns, sipping their coffee and looking out at the noisy thoroughfare that leads to a rocky cliff and down to the sea.

'Are you going out somewhere, *mama*?' Aneesa asks as she comes out on to the balcony one early morning.

Waddad is dressed in a black trouser suit and her hair is brushed back to reveal a well-scrubbed face. She pours Aneesa a cup of coffee.

'I've got lots to do today before I go to the orphanage.'

Aneesa sits down, picks up her cup and notices a pile of official-looking papers on the table. Waddad folds the papers and puts them in her handbag.

'It's just some business that I have to take care of, that's all,' she says.

'But maybe I can help you with it.'

Waddad takes a deep breath and looks anxiously at her daughter.

'I have to do this myself, Aneesa.'

'Will you tell me about it, please?'

'I read about it in the paper yesterday,' Waddad begins.

'What is it? What's happened?'

'They've passed the new law.'

Tears begin to fall down Waddad's face. Aneesa leans towards her but the older woman shakes her head.

'The one that gives the relatives of the missing the right to have them declared dead if they've been gone for more than seven years.'

Waddad sniffs loudly and pulls a tissue from beneath her sleeve cuff. Aneesa watches closely.

'Are you sure you want to do this? You do know what it means, *mama*?'

'It's been a long time now, *habibti*, nearly nine years.'

Is that why you're wearing black today, Aneesa wants to ask? It makes you look even smaller, almost like a child in adult's clothing.

Aneesa gazes at her mother, at the lines in her face and coarse, short hair and feels her own pain shift to another part of her body, to a permanent, deeper place.

'Just give me half an hour,' Aneesa says getting up. 'I'll dress and come with you.'

Ramzi tries at first to teach the bird to speak, simple words like marhaba or habibi or even his own name. But the bird just looks at him vacantly, its head jerking nervously from side to side, as if to say, You're asking too much of me. So Ramzi takes to whistling to it instead, tunes he has heard on the radio that plays in the orphanage kitchen during mealtimes and which he repeats again and again to the bird, or songs he remembers from home. He whistles, takes deep breaths, and looks into the cage at

*the tiny creature, at its curved beak and the neat fold of
its wings.*

*Soon, Ramzi begins to notice recognition in the bird's
eyes as he approaches, something in the way it suddenly
starts to flit along the length of its perch and the hint of
excitement in its insistent chirping. Until one day, as he
dresses to go down to breakfast, Ramzi hears his own
song coming from the cage on the windowsill, four notes
repeated again and again as if to call him nearer. He peers
into the cage and sings back to the bird in a low voice.
La, la, la, la, la.*

*Salah, whenever I think he is not looking, I observe
Ramzi closely but all I see is a sorry child adrift in
loneliness and misguided hope. Our elders here tell us
that in the forward movement of our souls is certain
salvation, limitless opportunities to stand nearer to the
true nature of our selves and to a forgiving god.*

The village is very much as Aneesa remembers it: old
stone houses alongside grey, concrete structures with
balconies and rusty clothes-lines hanging from their
balustrades. But the roads are better maintained and the
umbrella pine forests are there on the outskirts of the
village, visible and beautiful still.

She drives into the *souq* and stops the car by the village
spring.

'I'm getting us some water,' she says. 'Would either of
you like anything else?'

Waddad shakes her head.

'Can I come with you?' Ramzi asks from the back
seat.

'All right, come on.'

The spring water comes out of the spout in a thin murky rope. A lone woman bends down in front of it, filling a large blue plastic canister. Aneesa and Ramzi step into a musty-smelling, dark shop.

'*Ahlan*,' says a man from behind the counter.

'It's difficult to see in here.'

'The electricity's been cut off again,' says the man. 'Happens almost every day now.'

'I'll have three small bottles of water,' Aneesa says. 'Ramzi, why don't you get yourself some sweets?'

Ramzi absently reaches for a bar of chocolate and hands it to her.

'Is that all you want?'

He nods.

Aneesa grabs a handful of chocolates and several sticks of chewing gum.

'I think I'll get some for myself as well.'

Once outside, she takes two bars of chocolate out of the plastic bag and gives one to Ramzi. They busy themselves with opening the wrappers.

'Is this where you grew up, Aneesa?'

She shakes her head.

'No, I only came here in the summer as a child. It's my father's village. The rest of the year we lived in Beirut.'

'Your brother too?'

'Yes, Bassam did too. He didn't much like it here.'

They begin to make their way to the car.

'I'm from a village on the other side of the mountain,' Ramzi says. 'I wasn't born in the orphanage.'

'I know.'

'Aneesa?' He says her name softly. 'Do you think they like me there? At the orphanage, I mean?'

She hears a car start up at the other end of the square and the sound of running feet in the distance. She pats Ramzi on the arm and pushes him gently towards the car.

'Come on. *Mama*'s waiting.'

The drive up to the house takes only a few minutes.

'This' – Aneesa points through the windscreen – 'is our house.' The green shutters are closed and the plants in the garden are all dry and brown. 'Did you bring the key, *mama*?'

'Yes, I did. But I don't think we should go in.'

'Why not?' Aneesa takes the key from her mother and walks up to the front door. 'I want to show Ramzi Bassam's room. There'll be lots of things in there that he'd be interested in.'

She steps inside. Waddad grabs hold of Ramzi's arm as he attempts to follow Aneesa indoors.

'Ramzi doesn't need to go inside,' she says with urgency. 'I don't want him going in there.'

Ramzi looks at Aneesa and then back at Waddad.

'I'll stay out here with you,' he says to the older woman.

The house is dark and damp. Aneesa tiptoes through the rooms, afraid of recalling too much. Standing in the doorway of Bassam's old room, she suddenly understands her mother's fear. What if Ramzi remembered nothing at all? She hurries back to the front door, steps outside and locks it behind her.

In the back garden, Waddad and Ramzi are sitting on a stone ledge where the rose bushes had once been. Their heads are bent close together and they do not hear her approaching.

'Father was a good man,' Ramzi is saying. 'But he just didn't understand.'

Waddad nods, puts her hand through his arm and waits for him to continue.

'Bassam followed him around with that bucket whenever he pruned the roses, hoping to be praised for what he did, but all along the boy knew it was Aneesa his father wanted with him.'

We were in the house once and you told me you needed to have your hair cut. You picked up the newspaper on the coffee table and put your hand on the front of your shirt and patted your chest. I rummaged in my handbag and handed you a black ballpoint pen. I moved to the sofa and watched you draw a wide, oval-shaped arch on the corner of the paper where there was no print.

'This is what my hair should look like,' you said. 'On the right side, it's exactly right.' You turned your head and smoothed back your hair. 'See?'

I looked at you and nodded.

Then next to the first arch, you drew another, this time in a square shape.

'But on the other side, it's all wrong, like this,' you continued.

I stood up, crossed over in front of you and looked at your left profile.

'You're right,' I said.

'I know I need a haircut, but they can never seem to get it right here.' You put down your pen and shook your head. 'I miss my barber in Beirut.'

I put my head back and laughed loudly.

'Come to Beirut with me then,' I said. 'Come home

with me and we'll get your hair cut the way it should be.'

But when I looked back at you again, there was only sorrow in your face.

Aneesa does not remember the last time she saw Bassam. Instead, there is a persistent image in her mind of a day they spent together only a week before his abduction.

It is summer and they are at the beach in the south with a group of their friends. The fighting seems to have come to a temporary stop and the war is far from all their minds.

Bassam has brought with him a young woman whom Aneesa has not met before. She is petite and very pretty, with fair hair and startlingly green eyes. Bassam introduces her as Leila and the two spend much of their time sitting together on the sand or jostling each other at the edge of the water. Aneesa wonders if her brother has fallen in love. It is not something they have ever talked about and she feels a momentary distance from him, as if he has changed in some way, as if there are many things in his life that she does know about.

The sea is especially beautiful today because rather than being its usual still self in the heat of summer, Aneesa can see ripples of waves in the distance that move down to the shore lazily and end in a frothy foam on the wet sand. She watches Bassam and his friend step into the water and swim out into the distance. They come to a stop and move closer to one another so that their shiny heads seem to be touching. Aneesa looks away and turns on to her stomach and tries to listen to what a friend next to her is saying.

Later, as they prepare to leave, Leila comes up behind

the car where Aneesa is getting out of her bathing suit and putting on her clothes.

'Hello,' says the young woman. 'Do you mind if I get dressed here too?'

Aneesa shakes her head and pulls a blouse over her head. She does not look at Leila.

'We didn't really get a chance to talk, did we?' says Leila. 'Bassam has told me so much about you.'

Aneesa puts on her denims and takes a pair of sandals out of a plastic bag.

'I guess Bassam didn't tell you about me?' Leila's voice is quiet but when Aneesa looks at her she is smiling. 'We haven't known each other very long but I like him a lot. Maybe he doesn't feel the same about me?'

'I'm sure that's not why he hasn't mentioned you before,' Aneesa says hurriedly. 'He's just very private about things like this.'

Leila smiles.

'You're sweet,' she says, making Aneesa feel slightly embarrassed at the compliment.

When they've finished dressing, they walk away from the car and join the others once again. The sun is beginning to set and Aneesa feels a shiver run through her body. She looks around for Bassam and sees him coming out of the water.

'I can't believe he's still swimming,' Leila says with a shake of her head. 'He must be freezing. I'll take a towel out to him.'

Leila runs down towards Bassam waving with one hand and holding a towel with the other. Aneesa watches her brother's face. He is smiling. The sky above him is beginning to turn a slow, soft red and the sea is moving fluidly and silently behind him. He grabs the towel from Leila and wraps it quickly around his body, then he puts an arm over the young woman's shoulder and pulls her towards him. As Aneesa prepares to turn back to the car, Bassam looks up and waves to her. He cups his hands over his mouth and calls out.

'Aneesa!'

But she only turns and walks away.

Leila left the country only weeks after Bassam's disappearance and Aneesa never got the chance to talk to her about him. Now, she wonders what her brother had wanted to say to her on that day. Sometimes she thinks he had been trying to point to his own happiness on such a perfect day. At others, she imagines he had been about to say something of such significance that she would for ever remember it. But most of all, she will always be ashamed of having refused to share what might have been one of his final joyous moments.

PART TWO

When they come for him Bassam knows that there is no escape. He sees them standing at the front door with his mother as he comes out of his room. There are four of them, looking very ordinary, although the ringleader is dressed in fatigues. Bassam recognizes one man who stands in the hallway, half hidden by the door. He is short and thin with a bushy moustache and Bassam is certain he has seen him at one of the many political meetings he has attended. Perhaps he is the informer, Bassam says to himself as he approaches the men.

'*Ahlan, ahlan,*' he welcomes the men and puts his arm around Waddad's shoulders. They all shake hands and pretend to have a normal conversation. Bassam tells Waddad he must attend to some business and will wash and get changed before leaving. He hears her offering the men some coffee as he walks back to the bathroom.

In his room, Bassam looks around carefully at all his things: the unmade bed pushed against one wall just below the window; the too-big cupboard that nearly overwhelms the room; his cluttered desk and the clothes he took off last night and threw on to the chair. He does not think he has time to write to Aneesa to explain and he is concerned that if he delays in coming out the men might hurt his mother. He dresses quickly, pulling on a clean pair of trousers and shirt. He is surprised at how calm he feels, perhaps because he has been expecting this for some time now. He picks up a comb and runs it through his hair, then he looks at himself in the mirror. His face is pale and drawn with tiredness. He wishes suddenly that he were a child again and that the war had never been.

At the front door, Bassam gives Waddad a quick peck on the cheek and smiles broadly.

'Everything will be all right, *mama*,' he says quietly.

There is an anxious look on Waddad's face as he reaches to touch her hair. It is still long and silky though she has it held back in a bun.

'Take care, *habibti*,' Bassam whispers.

'What time are you coming home?' Waddad asks as he goes through the door with the men.

'Don't worry, *khalti*, he'll be back later,' the ringleader says with a chuckle as he puts his arm through Bassam's.

'Did you bring your car keys?' the ringleader asks Bassam once they get downstairs.

Bassam nods.

'Give them to me.' The ringleader throws the keys to one of the men. 'Follow us in his car. It's the little red Renault in the car park over there.'

'What do you want my car for?' Bassam asks but the man ignores him.

They lead him to a small van and tell him to climb

into the back. One man sits next to him. When he unzips his jacket, Bassam sees the gun pushed into the top of his trousers. The man takes a cigarette out of his pocket and lights it up without offering one to Bassam.

It is a sunny day and because it is still morning, people are out in the streets. The fighting doesn't usually begin until late in the afternoon once everyone is home from work and the militiamen have had their rest. It seems to Bassam, for one moment at least, that Beirut is back to its normal self, cars are hooting their horns at one another and there is a sense of buoyancy in the air. He laughs out loud and the man next to him looks up.

'Shut up,' the man says with obvious boredom.

Bassam shakes his head and looks out of the car window, suddenly wishing he had seen his sister before she left the house earlier that morning.

His father had always insisted that the family spend several weeks of the summer in their home in the mountains. But it was Aneesa who seemed to enjoy the experience most. Bassam remembers her as a little girl, dressed in a thin cotton dress and sandals, her legs slim and brown as she danced around the roses that their father had loved so much. There had been something baffling about her even then, a kind of wholeness that excluded everyone else. Still, he had felt fiercely protective of Aneesa when they were children and feels it even more strongly now that they are both older. The thought that he might have let his sister and mother down enters Bassam's head.

'Where are you taking me?' he asks, but no one bothers to reply.

*   *   *

There are many things that Bassam regrets. He was never particularly close to his father, perhaps because they were both too embarrassed to show affection openly; nor did he ever make a real effort to understand his mother, his role being only one of protector rather than friend. There have been times since his father's death, however, that Bassam has sensed in Waddad a strength greater than his own, a resourcefulness that makes him uneasy at times.

He is also sorry that he left university before he had gained a degree, something he knows he would never have done if his father had been alive. I might have had a chance, if I had continued, to eventually leave this country and find work, he thinks. I would have sent for mother and Aneesa later on and then we all might have been free.

Aneesa. It had been his maternal grandmother's name, soft and beautiful like his sister, the sweet companion, the friend. That is what Aneesa is to him, someone he can trust, who sees the things he fears most and loves him the only way she knows how, fiercely and without reproach.

'That's not the way you do it, Aneesa,' Bassam says, pushing his sister away impatiently. 'Here, let me.'

They are trying to put up a tent in the back garden of the house in the mountains. Their father has given them instructions on what to do but Bassam is not sure he has understood. He is feeling angry with himself and with Aneesa's futile fumbling with the pegs and ropes.

'It's no use you trying to do something you know nothing about,' he says with anger.

Aneesa looks at him and sighs.

'I'll go and get some cushions for us to sit on inside the tent,' she says. 'You put it up, Bassam, and I'll be right back.'

She skips as she moves, her body light and delicate. For a moment he imagines she might float away from him and up into the pine trees.

Bassam eventually calls his father to help him pitch the tent, so that when Aneesa comes back, her arms full of cushions, it is up, its two flap doors pulled back to invite them in. She claps her hands and the cushions fall on the ground.

'I knew you could do it, Bassam,' she squeals with delight. 'Isn't it beautiful, *baba*?'

He is not sure why he did not confide in her about his political activities. It was partly because he feared for her safety but there was something else also. Perhaps, Bassam admits to himself, I wanted to do something that she would not be a part of; something that would give me the sense of being free and independent.

Bassam hangs his head and for the first time since his capture feels fear, not just for himself but for everyone, his mother and his sister, for these sorry men who are as mindless as the wretched war they insist on making.

He is being held with about a dozen other men in an old building near the city sports centre. There are armed militiamen at the entrance to the building and in the hallway outside the room where the prisoners are kept. The room is large but has no windows and a group of men are sitting on cushions on the floor. The air is heavy with smoke and someone lights a cigarette when Bassam walks in. He stands there for a moment looking for a familiar face when one of the men motions to him to come and share his cushion.

'The floor is cold,' says the man quietly, though he does not smile. 'You'll be better off here.'

'Thank you.'

Bassam leans his back against a wall and looks around. Some of the prisoners seem to have been here for several days. They look bedraggled and sleepy.

'They brought me in yesterday and still haven't told me what's going on,' the man next to Bassam says with a sigh. 'I was on my way back home from work and was stopped at a checkpoint. I work down at the port.'

Bassam nods but does not say anything.

'What about you? Does your family know what has happened to you?'

Before Bassam can reply, the door opens and an armed man appears, dragging someone in behind him. The detainee falls on to the floor and moans loudly. Nobody moves until the guard shuts the door again.

'He's been badly beaten,' one of the prisoners says as he leans over the injured man.

When they lift him, the man moans again. They move him to a corner of the room and put his head on a cushion. Someone puts a jacket over him.

'Does anyone have any water?'

One of the men takes a small plastic bottle out of his pocket.

'I saved this from this morning,' he says as he hands the bottle over.

The injured man sips at the water and closes his eyes.

Bassam's companion shakes his head.

'So, does your family have any idea that you've been taken?' he asks again.

'They came for me at home. Walked up to my front door, greeted my mother and asked me to go with them.' Bassam shrugs his shoulders. 'I never thought they'd be as bold as that.'

'It happens all the time,' says the man. 'If they want to get you, believe me, they'll find you.'

'Had they been looking for you too?'

The man shakes his head.

'I was in the wrong place at the wrong time, I suppose. The militiaman at the barricade didn't like the sound of my name.' He smiles and looks at Bassam. 'The funny thing is, I've been all right all this time, escaped the worst of the bombardments, and now this! What Allah wills is bound to happen. There is nothing we can do.'

Some time later, when he looks at his watch, Bassam realizes it is early evening and the fighting outside has resumed. He can hear gunfire and the occasional mortar fire at some distance. He wonders what Waddad and Aneesa are thinking now that he has not returned home. I should have let them know something like this might happen, he thinks.

He had been involved with the party for nearly two years. The leadership promised great things, that together they would put a stop to the rule of the militias and allow people to live normal lives again, although all those promises sound too good to be true now. Bassam felt when he was approached to join the group that he had no choice. He was young and strong and without a job or prospects for the future. It was either become a member of a political group or emigrate and there was no way he could have gone away and left his mother and sister on their own in the midst of this madness. I did what I had to do, he nods to himself.

The man next to him is snoring with his back up against the wall. Bassam slides down so that his head is on the cushion, wraps his jacket more tightly around him and tries to fall asleep.

His father comes to him in a dream. He looks different, with a full head of hair, and he is much taller than he was in real life. A young Bassam walks alongside him, occasionally looking up to catch what he is saying. They are in search of their flat and want to return home and though they seem to be going in the right direction – Bassam recognizes the road leading up to the block, cliffs going down to the water on one side and the wide esplanade on the other – they cannot find it.

They sit down eventually, on a large grey rock that has moss all over it. Bassam jumps up and examines the seat of his trousers which is now covered with seaweed. When he looks around him, he realizes that he is standing on the Raouche Rock, high up above the water. Beyond is the horizon. His father stands at the edge of the rock but when Bassam approaches him he disappears. Down in the water, there is no sign of anyone having fallen in. Bassam raises his head to the sky and there is his father, floating up into the clouds so that eventually Bassam only sees the soles of his feet, two dark imprints in a sky of white.

He wakes up stiff with cold. The man next to him is still snoring and most of the others are still asleep. He walks to the door and knocks softly and is surprised when it opens.

'What is it?' the guard asks him.

'I need the toilet.'

The guard looks at him closely and shrugs, then he takes him by the arm, pulls him out of the room and locks the door again. Bassam realizes that he is not the same militiaman who was at the door earlier. In the dim light of the single bulb in the hallway there is a small kitten at the man's feet. Its head is bent over a scrap of newspaper where morsels of cheese have been placed.

'Its mother must have been run over by a car,' the man whispers to Bassam. 'I picked it up on my way over here. Poor thing was starving.'

Bassam looks at the militiaman. He is young, with dark hair and eyes. He could be any one of the dozens of people Bassam meets in the streets every day, and although there is a certain gentleness in his face, he carries his machine gun with the ease of long experience.

'It's good of you to take care of it,' Bassam finally says.

The man looks at him and nods.

'It's that one on the left,' he says, pointing behind him. 'Two minutes only. And leave the door open.'

In the morning, the man sitting next to Bassam is summoned away by the guard. He looks anxious as he walks out of the room, but when he returns moments later, he is smiling.

'My brother-in-law has come for me,' he tells Bassam. 'He knows the leader here and they told him there'd been some mistake. It was someone else they were after.' He grabs his jacket and puts out his other hand. 'Do you want me to get a message to someone for you? Give me your mother's number. I'll telephone her if you like.'

'We have not even exchanged names,' Bassam says, shaking the man's hand. He imagines Waddad receiving the call and trying desperately to do something, even coming out here to find him. He shakes his head. 'It's all right,' he says. 'I'm sure I'll be out soon, anyway. Thank you.'

Once his companion has left, Bassam looks around him. The man who was beaten last night is sitting up. His face is bruised and there is dried blood on one side of his head but he seems otherwise all right. He looks at Bassam and blinks before turning away.

The door opens and the guard comes in again. It is the same man who was at the door when Bassam had arrived the day before.

'You,' the guard yells, pointing at Bassam. 'Come here.'

He grabs Bassam by his collar and pulls him through into the hallway, then he pushes him roughly into a room several doors down. Bassam lands on the floor. When he looks up he sees another militiaman standing above him.

'Here's our hero,' the man says loudly and kicks Bassam in the stomach. 'Have you come to save this country from evil? Is that what you have in mind?'

The man walks away and then turns around again. Bassam waits for his own breath to return.

'Pull him up,' the man says to the guard.

Once Bassam is standing, the man looks closely at him. 'What do you think is going to happen to you?' he asks.

Bassam shakes his head.

'I don't know,' he says quietly.

'You are an enemy,' the leader shouts into Bassam's face. 'There is no place for you or your friends in this country.'

'This is my country,' Bassam says before he can stop himself.

The man slaps him. Bassam falls to the floor once again.

'Put him back with the others,' he hears the militiaman telling the guard. 'I'll deal with him later.'

Later that night, after he has eaten a *labne* sandwich that one of the other detainees gave him, Bassam sits down on the cushion with his back against the wall and tries to look into a distance that isn't there. He thinks again of his mother and of Aneesa, and of Leila too whom he has not yet had a chance to love. He feels his heart clench inside him and the blood rush to his neck and up into his face.

Bassam begins to understand that the prospects of his getting away from here are not very good and wonders if he shouldn't just resign himself to his fate. After all, many thousands before him have died in the fighting and countless others are sure to follow before it is all over. He tries to imagine what Lebanon will be like after the war but finds it difficult. Will they forget what happened and simply get on with life, he wonders, or will the memory of it remain in the thoughts and minds of those who suffered most? If I die, he thinks to himself, Waddad will never forgive me and Aneesa will hold the injustice of it close to her heart, but will the reality of all this, the horror of it, remain with them?

Someone coughs. Bassam tries to focus his eyes in the now dark room and is comforted by the sound of the breathing of his fellow inmates.

He believes there is something so fantastic about war, about the fervent violence it engenders, that makes it almost unbelievable even when one is thrown in the midst of it. It is not fear, he says silently to himself, that makes me think I will somehow wake up and find my life is as it once was, tranquil and moving towards a gentle end; nor is it an attempt to deny what is happening to me. Rather, Bassam thinks as he slides down to rest his head on the cushion, it is the certainty that this war is as fragile and impermanent as the people who make it and will never be a part of truth that he has always known.

The next morning, the militiaman who interrogated Bassam the day before walks into the room and motions to him to follow.

'Go get his car,' the man tells the guard once they are outside. 'Have one of the men follow us in the jeep. This guy is going for a ride.'

Bassam is sitting in the back seat of his own car with a gunman on either side of him. His hands have been tied in front of him but he is glad that they have not blindfolded him as well. It is mid-morning and the sky is cloudy and grey but there is no rain. He smells the stench of exhaust fumes through one of the car windows. Perhaps if he had left the keys behind in his bedroom they would not have taken this car away and Aneesa could have used it. His head is aching a little. The driver is going fast and Bassam is thrown roughly against the men beside him. He thinks of reaching over to open the door and jumping out but decides he would not get away with it. There must be some way of escaping, he thinks, maybe once the car comes to a stop. We're bound to encounter some traffic.

'How much longer?' the militiaman sitting next to Bassam asks.

The gunman sitting in the front snorts loudly.

'We'll get there soon enough,' he says.

Bassam looks out of the window once again. The people walking around in these streets, he thinks, are just as much prisoners of this war as I am.

He wishes he had some way of telling Waddad and Aneesa that he is all right, that one day soon he will come back to see them.

PART THREE

PART THREE

Aneesa has found a small flat in a quiet neighbourhood in the northwest part of the London. There is one bedroom, a shower room and a kitchen that opens out on to a rectangular living space with a large window overlooking the street. She has a bed and an armchair and a sofa in the way of furniture and enough crockery and silverware for her limited needs. Her translation work is done at a small table that she has placed between the kitchen and the living room and which she also uses to have her meals.

The novelty of having her own place, however small, does not wear off, even months after moving into the flat. On the telephone to her mother, Aneesa tries to tone down the excitement in her voice because she does not want Waddad to think that she is happier far away than she had been at home. But there are times when she questions if she was not always meant to live like this, so alone that the edges of her self are bristling and sharp in her encounters with others and at night when she tucks herself into bed and lies breathing in the dark. And then there is the crushing absence of sunlight. It is almost as if this new world, grey and faltering, invites ambiguity, calls her to a place where she has no identity and where nothing is clearly defined.

The company she freelances for is a half-hour bus ride from home. On the days she is required to go to the office, she takes a secret delight in waking early, in dressing carefully and going out into the morning like so many other commuters, standing silently at the bus stop and stamping her feet in the cold. Whenever it rains, she carries a large umbrella that she brought with her from Beirut and which she soon realizes was meant to keep out the sun rather than rainfall. She grows adept at shaking the umbrella out before stepping on to the bus or going indoors, tucking it expertly under her arm afterwards and remembering to take it with her when she leaves. She wonders how long it will be before she feels completely a part of this place, before it becomes where she comes from and everything she knows rather than somewhere she has merely been.

On one of her visits to the office, Aneesa meets Isabel, also a translator. She is red-haired and tall and the kind of person who fills up a room as soon as she walks into it. Isabel greets everyone and looks straight at Aneesa who is sitting at a desk making some final changes to a document she has been working on.

'You're the new Arabic translator, aren't you?' she asks.

Aneesa nods and smiles.

'Hi, I'm Isabel. I do French and German.'

Aneesa stands up and puts out her hand.

'What's your name?' Isabel asks.

'Aneesa.'

The two women shake hands.

After work, they go out for a meal at a café in a nearby department store. They choose sandwiches and drinks from the food counter and sit at a table by the window that looks out on to the street. Aneesa still feels shy but has begun to warm towards this vibrant woman.

'I suppose you come into the office for a bit of company just like I do?' Isabel asks between mouthfuls.

Aneesa is startled at the question.

'Don't look so shocked,' Isabel laughs. 'I know how difficult it is to be a single woman in this city because I've been one for years. It's the ambivalence that gets to me, though. I like being on my own but there are moments when I want to be completely surrounded by people.'

Aneesa feels comforted at having her own feelings expressed so clearly but says nothing.

'Do you have family here?'

'Just a relative of my mother's who helped me come here and find work,' Aneesa says. 'I haven't been here very long. My mother lives in Beirut.'

'Terrible war over there. It's a good thing you got out in one piece.'

Aneesa looks down at her own food, picks up a crisp and pops it into her mouth. She crunches it slowly, savouring the saltiness and the sharp sting of vinegar. She looks at Isabel as she eats, notices the freckles on the bridge of her nose and across her cheeks, her hazel eyes

91

and her small, pink ears that are almost hidden beneath the mane of long hair.

'Where are you from?' Aneesa asks.

'I was born here but my mother is French and I went to a German school, hence the languages. I studied translation at university and here I am. It's good money and I like working from home and keeping my own hours. What's your third language, by the way?'

'French, like most Lebanese. We all have to learn it, along with English, at school. My father was an English Literature professor at the Lebanese University. That's where I got my degree in translation. I worked for a number of years back home before coming here.'

She realizes she has not talked so much about herself since she first came here, and the discovery makes her heart race a little.

'So you must be in your early thirties, like me?' Isabel asks without waiting for a reply. 'That's good.'

It is a pleasant chat, filled with the kind of innocuous, friendly conversation that Aneesa has not really had in a long time. She is heartened at the thought that this young woman does not see her as being in any way different from herself and hopes they will see each other again.

When they're finished eating, Isabel asks Aneesa for her telephone number.

'I'm having some friends over for drinks at the weekend and I'd like you to come. I'll call you and let you know where it is.'

Aneesa has taken to talking to herself. On a crowded bus returning home, a carrier bag in one hand and her handbag in another, she stands precariously between seats and repeats to herself what she must do next, so quietly that she is certain no one can hear her. Up the steps to the flat and then sort out the groceries; remember the fish is for tonight and the yoghurt for breakfast tomorrow; the bus is coming to a stop, hold on to something now or you'll keel over. Sometimes she whispers a secret resolve as she walks down the street or while sitting in a café at the weekend: I will not despair, I will be strong. But there are days when no matter how hard she tries to feign the vague lack of concern she has noticed in people here, there is no escaping thoughts of home. She telephones her mother and tries to detect a plea for her to return but there is none.

'Are you sure you're all right, *mama*?' Aneesa asks. 'I feel so terrible about being far away when you need me most.'

'*Habibti*, I love you more than you'll ever know but I can manage very well on my own,' Waddad replies in a matter-of-fact voice. 'All you're feeling is guilt, Aneesa. It's time you grew out of that. You have a right to a life of your own.'

It is new, this learning how to separate herself from people and circumstances that are no longer there. How do I become whole, Aneesa asks herself? How does it feel on the inside, this single pursuit, this self-delineated path?

She watches Isabel who seems to float effortlessly in a cloud of activity and purpose. They meet often now, together or along with an ever-changing group of men and women whom Isabel describes as her friends. Aneesa joins them when they go out to trendy restaurants and bars, eat, drink and talk about themselves, what they are doing now and what they hope to do in the future. Her new friends are from everywhere and nowhere in particular, rudderless, as if they had been planted here by an invisible hand and might easily vanish without warning or consequence. For Aneesa, they are the ideal companions, asking nothing of her other than that she be entertaining and equally as preoccupied as they are. And for a while, this is what makes her happy.

When she finally reached adolescence, Aneesa's world had begun to appear narrower, not because others in it had suddenly grown larger but because she herself, the essential parts of her that were exclusively her own and which could not be mistaken for anyone else, had become more intense, more persistent. The almost palpable reality of this change had taken her by surprise and made her feel awkward around the people she had once been so comfortable with, her family and friends and all those who ventured in and out of an existence that seemed entirely of her own making.

Now as she attempts to adjust to a new life, Aneesa recognizes similarities to those earlier years. But this time there is gratification associated with her separateness, a sense that she has finally gained control over her destiny and that it is her will alone that can direct it.

'You've never had a boyfriend, have you?' Isabel asks Aneesa one day. They are sitting on the sofa in Aneesa's living room drinking tea and flipping through fashion magazines.

'No.' Aneesa is long past trying to evade Isabel's questions. 'I mean there were those boys at school but nothing serious.'

'But what about at university and afterwards at work? How did you manage to avoid it?'

Aneesa has not told Isabel about losing a brother.

'My father died and I had to take care of my mother. I just didn't have time.'

'Mind you, they're pretty conservative where you come from, aren't they? Don't approve of pre-marital sex, I suppose.'

Aneesa does not reply.

'I'm sorry,' says Isabel softly. 'I don't mean to be insensitive but don't you think it's time you found someone you can become close to? It doesn't have to be a permanent thing, you know. I just think you're missing out, that's all.'

Sometime later, Isabel tells Aneesa there is someone she wants her to meet, and repeats this several times over the next few weeks.

'Who is he?' Aneesa finally asks.

'Just someone I've known for a long time,' Isabel replies with a smile. 'I have a feeling you'll get along.'

When Aneesa first meets Robert she does not expect to like him. He is tall and fair and smiles at her with the confidence of one who expects to be admired. As the evening progresses, however, she finds herself talking to him with ease, like someone long familiar.

'I've been to Lebanon you know,' he says. 'I was part of a film crew shooting a documentary on the war. I made several visits and must have spent a couple of months there altogether.'

'Is that what you do, then?' she asks. 'Make films?'

'I work mostly as a producer now. I started out as a cameraman, though.'

He does not pursue the subject of Lebanon, nor does he ask her why she left or whom she has left behind, and she realises that that unquestioning acceptance is exactly what she wants from him.

When Robert reaches for her later that night, cupping her face in both his hands and bending down to kiss her, she watches his eyes darken as he gets closer, sees the longing in them and is surprised to feel it too.

This is not love, Aneesa reminds herself, just something like it, something real yet containable, a quiet interlude that pleases her and leaves her wanting more. Robert is lovely and fun and sometimes with her but more often away for work. The arrangement suits her perfectly. She feels settled in it, balanced and predictable in the way that the elements can be during any given year. She cherishes her solitude and only longs for him once he returns.

She does not tell her mother about Robert. Waddad seems immersed in concerns of her own, seeming further away than the distance that separates them. Their telephone conversations are most often short and stilted. And whenever Aneesa suggests returning at least for a visit, her mother tells her to wait a little longer, until things have settled a bit and the situation has improved.

'*Mama*, I hope you're being careful.' Aneesa feels suddenly anxious and remembers the heavy pall of the war. 'Please tell me you're not taking any unnecessary chances during the fighting.'

'Honestly,' Waddad replies, 'you're becoming like all the rest of the Lebanese living overseas. You know very well we just have to get on with things. I'm fine and yes, I am being careful.'

Aneesa wishes she could confide in her mother, tell her about her lover and the quietness that now envelops her life but cannot bring herself to do so. She does not try to work out why she should feel this way and decides simply to trust her instincts about it.

In time, Aneesa finds herself telling Robert about her father and about Bassam and the desperation she had felt after his abduction. He listens and holds her and does not offer any words of comfort or question her further. She likes this about him, his ability to absorb what she says without pity or surprise and the way he can later behave as though nothing between them has changed. When she looks at Robert during unguarded moments, as he sleeps or while he is busy concentrating on a difficult task, she cannot help but question how Bassam would have felt about him. She remembers the journalist her brother introduced her to in Beirut long ago and wonders if Bassam would have felt the same about the man who is now so close to his sister. Sometimes, she likes to imagine them together, Robert and Bassam sitting down on the sofa in her living room, watching her as she moves above the kitchen and smiling at her with equal measures of amusement and affection.

Almost a year after they first meet, Robert turns up unexpectedly at Aneesa's flat from one of his trips overseas. He pulls her into his arms before stepping inside.

'Things must have gone well on this trip,' Aneesa says,

hugging him back and realizing how much she has been looking forward to his return. 'Come on in, Robert. I've missed you.'

His face is flushed and he looks excited.

'Will you have something to eat?' Aneesa asks. 'I was just about to prepare some dinner.' She goes into the kitchen and begins to take some vegetables out of the refrigerator.

'I'm not hungry, Aneesa,' Robert calls out to her. 'I need to talk to you. Come and sit down.'

She joins him on the sofa and feels the warmth from his body enveloping her.

'What is it that's so urgent, Robert?' She smiles at him and shakes her head.

'You know that job I told you about before I left?' Robert begins. 'The one in New York that I had been hoping to get?'

Aneesa nods.

'Well, I've been offered it and they want me to go there right away. There was a message on my answerphone when I got back.'

'That's wonderful news, *habibi*,' Aneesa says, giving him a hug. 'I'm so happy for you.' She feels a twinge of anxiety before she asks him when he is due to leave.

'There's a lot to organize over here first. I have to sort out my flat and we'll have to find work over there for you as well. And I'm sure we'll have no problem renting this flat before you follow me out there.'

'This flat?'

'Well, you won't want to keep it while you're away. We could be in America for some time.'

Aneesa stands up and looks down at him.

'Robert, what are you talking about?'

He reaches for her hand and grasps it.

'As soon as I heard about the job, I realized that there was no way I could leave without you,' he says after a pause. 'I love you, Aneesa.'

In all the time that they have been seeing each other, they have not really spoken of a future together and although Aneesa has sometimes wondered how long the relationship will endure, she has never felt the need to approach the subject with Robert.

'You've never said that before,' she says quietly.

'I thought you knew.' Robert stands up and reaches for her hand. 'It's taken me a long time to realize it, I know, but I'm very certain of how I feel.'

When she does not respond, he wraps his arms around her and whispers into her ear.

'We can get married before we leave, if that's what you want.'

For a moment, Aneesa does not know what to say.

'I didn't say anything about wanting to get married.' She pulls away from him and sits down again.

'We can go to Beirut first. It's time I met your mother anyway.'

Aneesa is surprised at how resentful she suddenly feels.

'My mother doesn't know about you, Robert,' she blurts out.

For the first time since she's known him, a look of pain crosses his face.

'You haven't told her about me?'

She shakes her head but says nothing.

'You don't love me, do you?' he asks after a long pause.

The finality of his words shocks her. Still, she cannot bring herself to say anything to comfort him.

'Robert, I never realized this was how you felt. I—'

He lifts a hand to stop her.

'Please, don't say anything more. I'll leave now.'

'Robert, don't go. Let's talk, please.'

He shakes his head and opens the front door and she does not try to stop him from walking away.

Tonight, Bassam and her father are ghosts in her dream and everything around them, the faint light that illuminates their movements and the distant sounds that accompany their voices, appears ethereal, as if they would all disappear with a single flutter of her eyelid. And even as she dreams, Aneesa senses a strong desire to keep her father and brother there, to hold on to their awareness of each other and of herself floating somewhere in the background.

They are standing on the balcony of the flat in Beirut and are looking downwards; Bassam is calling out to someone on the ground below. She can see only the back of her father's head and Bassam, when he turns to look at him, appears vague too, although his features are accurate and clear. Hurry up, Bassam says. You've got to hurry and come up here.

When Aneesa follows the line of Bassam's vision, she sees a miniature, almost cartoon-like version of herself looking towards them and waving. She is so small that only her face, framed by dark, untamed hair, and her hand are visible. The moment that this unreal figure attempts to speak, everything around her begins to fade into the background until the final image, the single impression that is left behind is one of solid emptiness.

Aneesa wakes up and slowly opens her eyes but the darkness around her does not waver.

Aneesa does not see Robert again after that final argument but she does hear about his leaving for New York. She is also surprised when she stops hearing from Isabel. When she no longer comes across her friend at work, she telephones and leaves messages for her to call back. But Isabel never does.

Sometime later, Aneesa manages to get in touch with Isabel and the two women agree to meet at a café near work.

'I've missed you,' Aneesa begins.

'I've been away,' Isabel says.

'Oh.'

Isabel is absently stirring sugar into her coffee. She is not looking at Aneesa and seems reluctant to talk.

'What happened, Isabel? Are you angry with me about Robert? Please tell me what I've done.'

Isabel looks furiously back at her.

'Did you think he had no feelings, is that it?'

'I didn't know he was so serious about our relationship—'

'Aneesa, how could you possibly not know? It was obvious that he was very much in love with you.'

'Is that what it feels like? I didn't know.'

'Oh, don't play naïve with me, Aneesa. You're too old for that. You just didn't want to make a commitment. It wasn't convenient.'

'What do you mean?'

Isabel's anger seems suddenly to dissipate. She takes a deep breath.

'You've never taken us seriously, Aneesa, not me or Robert or any of us,' she says. 'We're just something new and exotic, something for you to discover and pretend to care about.'

'But I do care about you and Robert.' Aneesa is crying. Isabel reaches for her hand.

'I know you do, but not so much that it can hurt in any way. You've never really been here, Aneesa. In your head, you're always somewhere else.' Isabel pushes her chair back and stands up. 'You didn't hear from me for a while because I was in New York with Robert. He came to me after you left him. He was heartbroken.'

Sometimes, in the early evenings of her Western sojourn, Aneesa remains at home dressed in a pair of flannel pyjamas and a warm dressing gown and thinks she could live like this for the rest of her life. She moves around the flat in cloth slippers, preparing dinner and taking note of every step she takes. Aneesa, you are washing your hands now, she muses; after that you'll chop the carrots. Now you can switch the stove off and now it's time to do the dishes.

After eating, she picks up a book and holds it tightly to her chest as she makes her way to the living room. Once in a while, she might walk over to the window and pull the curtains back to glance at the grey street below.

But when she sits down on the sofa, just as she begins to get comfortable, an image of Waddad, alone in her apartment, comes to mind. She sits at the kitchen table, her head bent over a large tray covered with brown lentils. With the fingers of her right hand she removes small stones and bits of dirt which she then pushes to one side with her left hand. She has on her blue-framed reading glasses and her long grey hair is tied back with a black velvet ribbon. When she looks up, her eyes squinting through the lenses, Aneesa notices that her mother's skin is more tired than she remembered it. It is lined and soft and papery, as though covered with a thin film of powder.

PART FOUR

PART FOUR

S alah awaits a new-found happiness. At seventy-six, he is reluctant to appear to be searching for it, looking secretly for an indication of unexpected joys in everything that happens to him, in every encounter and despite the confines of his increasingly fragile life.

But since his arrival in this new city, he is careful not to show signs of his expectations to Samir, choosing instead to maintain the air of quiet resignation that his son has come to expect of him.

'What are you planning to do today then, Father?' Samir would ask before leaving for work, his body already leaning eagerly towards the front door.

'Oh, don't worry about me,' Salah would reply, looking up with a rueful smile and a gentle nod of the head. 'I've got plenty to keep me busy right here.'

Then, as soon as Samir has stepped outside, Salah would place the breakfast dishes in the dishwasher, run a cloth over the kitchen counters and rush upstairs to get ready to go out.

He dresses carefully, pulling on his trousers while sitting on the edge of the bed and buttoning the cuffs of his shirt before putting on socks and shoes. Then, experiencing a sudden frisson of excitement as he puts on his jacket and locks the front door behind him, Salah sets out for adventure.

At eighteen, Salah enters the American University of Beirut and spends his first few months there taking English language courses to prepare for the years of study ahead. He meets many young men like himself whose excellent grades in high school have secured them a place at the best university in the region.

There are women students at the university also. This is a new experience for Salah who has spent his childhood in boys' schools. Although some of the women are natives of Lebanon like himself, most of them are foreign, either from other Arab countries like Iraq, Palestine or Syria, or from as far as Europe and America.

He continues to live with his parents and two sisters in an apartment building in Ras Beirut that is only minutes away from the university. Both his sisters are younger than he is and are still at school. Although Salah does not know it yet he comes from an enlightened family for whom education is a priority for both sons and daughters. His parents are distant relatives and have lived in Beirut all their lives but they have instilled in him a respect for the world and all it has to offer and have encouraged in him the desire to widen his horizons.

A few weeks into the term a neighbour, an old woman who takes in foreign students, asks Salah if he will accompany one of her lodgers to her classes.

'She is from India and arrived late in the term,' the neighbour tells Salah. 'She does not know her way around and is feeling a little anxious. I thought it would be nice if you walked her to the university just for the first week or so, until she's got used to things.'

The young woman is very pretty, with long, dark hair and big eyes. She shakes Salah's hand slowly. It feels very soft to the touch.

'My name is Sita,' she says with a smile.

But Salah is too shy to reply.

They walk side by side on the street parallel to the one where the university is situated. Salah has decided to take a slightly circuitous route so that he can study Sita further. She has a plain dress on but there are gold bangles on her right wrist that jangle as she moves and her hair is braided so that it falls flat and thick against her back. He thinks perhaps he will help her when they cross the street to protect her from oncoming trams and motorcars.

'What is your name?' she asks as they prepare to cross the street.

Salah holds on to the young woman's arm and hopes he is not squeezing too tightly.

'Salah,' he says under his breath once they get to the other side. He lets go of Sita's arm.

They are approaching the fig tree by the hospital where Salah's mother had a small operation only months before. Once they're past that, they'll turn left and go down towards the main university entrance. Salah is aware that he is nervous but cannot understand why. Suddenly, he hears Sita cry out.

'Oh, no!'

He is right behind her as she collapses into his arms. He takes one or two steps backwards but still manages to hold on to her. He looks at her face. Her skin has gone grey and her eyelids are fluttering. She is leaning heavily against him and there is nothing he can do but wait for her to recover. Moments later, Sita pushes herself up and tries to stand straight. Salah holds her by the shoulders and tells her to take a deep breath.

'Are you all right?' he asks nervously.

The young woman nods and, pointing across the street, turns her head away with a loud sob. Salah follows the direction of her finger to the butcher shop where a sheep has just been slaughtered, its head lying intact beside its lifeless body.

'It's barbaric,' Sita says through her tears.

But Salah can think only of the feel of her body against his own, the suppleness of it and of the realization that it had disturbed him. A few days later, he finds out that Sita has returned home to India.

He spends much of his time indoors at first, going out only when Samir returns from work and the two of them would walk to the high street for some groceries or for a quick meal at the corner café. Eventually, Salah feels brave enough to go out on his own for a walk to the park or down to the train station to watch commuters pushing their weight through the turnstiles and scurrying up and down the stairs.

He discovers a new freedom in anonymity, in the studied indifference of the strangers who walk past him, their eyes pointing straight ahead, their stride confident and uninterrupted. It is also there in the apparent endlessness of this huge city, unbroken movement and a luring promise of novelty in its buzzing streets. He grows increasingly confident, venturing beyond the immediate neighbourhood of the house on most days, even risking a quiet hello at the newsagent's where he buys his Arabic newspaper on the way home.

When Samir arrives from work one day and hands him a bus pass, Salah examines it slowly, rubbing a finger over the photograph he'd had taken at the automatic machine inside the railway station a few days before.

'It's free, wherever you want to go,' Samir says, flashing a rare smile, both arms held wide open in front of him.

He begins to take buses everywhere, looking at the sign on the front of each of them as it approaches and quietly mouthing the strange-sounding names as he prepares to step on. He goes across town and back, through bustling commercial districts and untidy neighbourhoods that are very unlike the one he now lives in. He begins to feel as if the city has several hearts that beat separately, each at the centre of its own world.

Standing at the front door one chilly morning as he prepares to go out, Salah looks down the now familiar street, into the distance, and thinks of the roads back home that twist in and out of one another without apparent purpose, leading to untold journeys, catching sunlight in their wake.

'Do we live in the suburbs?' he asks Samir that evening.

'No, of course not. We're right in the centre of town. You should know that by now, *baba*.'

* * *

111

While Salah has always excelled at athletics – his slim shape and long limbs help him run and jump with ease – the one thing he cannot do is swim. It is a source of constant embarrassment to him during his days at university since he is loath to admit that his body betrays him in some way.

One day, Salah's athletics instructor decides to take his students to the beach.

'We'll do a few laps and play some games in the water,' the instructor tells them. 'It encourages flexibility and endurance.'

Salah makes his way down to the stretch of rocky beach that is also part of the campus with a sinking heart. Once there, Salah is momentarily distracted by the activity around him. He and his fellow students have changed into their swimming suits and are standing on the concrete platform that abuts the water. Around them are dozens of other young men and women either lying down on towels or standing around chatting or splashing noisily in the sea.

'Right, all of you, get in and swim up to the plank over there and back,' the instructor suddenly belts out. 'No dawdling now.'

Floating on top of the water a short distance from the shore is a platform with several students sitting on it. The platform does not look too far away and Salah thinks he might be able to make it that far if he can rest at the other end. He slips into the water and waits for his classmates to move ahead of him, then, slowly letting go of the concrete ledge, he begins a reluctant dog paddle. For a moment or two, Salah thinks he will be all right but as he moves further away from the shore, a panic suddenly overtakes him and he imagines he is being pulled downwards into the depths of the sea. His head goes down and he struggles to lift it up again. He splashes his arms and calls for help and out of nowhere, an arm appears and lifts his head up above the water. Salah feels his muscles suddenly relax and realizes he was only moments from drowning. His rescuer holds on to him until the instructor, now surrounded by a group of students, lifts him out of the water and on to the concrete slab where he is standing. Salah sits up and begins to cough. Someone taps him gently on the back.

'Are you all right?'

He looks round and into the face of the woman who rescued him. She is smiling and he notices that her eyes are green and her lashes sparkle with sea water. Salah breathes hard and manages to nod in answer to her question.

'He must have had cramp or something,' the young woman tells the instructor. 'He was doing fine until I saw him go down.'

'Just rest there for a while.' The instructor bends down and pats Salah on the back. 'I'll get the others and we'll head back to campus.'

Salah has never felt so ashamed and wishes the young woman would go and leave him on his own for a while.

'My name is Huda,' she says with a chuckle in her voice. 'What's yours?'

'Salah. I . . . Thank you.'

'I could teach you, you know.'

'Teach me?' Salah looks up at her again.

'You'd only need one or two lessons. Then next time you come here with your classmates, no one will know you couldn't swim before.'

*   *   *

The brown suede jacket lies on the bed. Samir bought it for him during a Saturday shopping spree that had included lunch and a walk across the park. It is the kind of thing that Salah would never have thought of buying when Huda was still alive. Too young for you, she would have said, smiling, before putting it back on the rack and reaching for something a little more staid, in blue and green plaid or dark charcoal with fine grey stripes.

As a young woman, Huda had black hair and skin so fair that everything she wore seemed only to intensify the contrast between them. She was slightly older than Salah and, on first meeting her, he had admired her confidence and her sensual grace and the muted assurance that pervaded everything she did.

He hangs his head and caresses the soft leather. Then he gets up, stands in front of the mirror and pulls on the jacket, zipping it up over the camel-hair scarf he bought to go underneath it.

At the graduation ceremony, Salah's family, his parents and sisters, stand waiting for him after all the diplomas have been handed out. His father, Salah knows, is disappointed that his son had not studied medicine but a diploma in civil engineering is a great achievement, nonetheless.

The family takes turns hugging and kissing Salah.

'We're proud of you, *habibi*,' they all say.

Then his father tells him they must talk.

'How would you like to travel for a few months after all your hard work? Your mother and I have arranged for you to go on a tour of Europe with a friend of the family. He's not much older than you are and has spent time travelling there and will be able to show you around.'

Salah is not sure what to think. He imagines himself standing on the deck of a ship gazing at a disappearing shoreline, but he cannot conjure images of foreign countries in his mind. He feels excitement bubble up inside him.

It is at this moment that he sees Huda approach with a couple whom he assumes must be her parents. She is wearing a soft green dress that matches her eyes and her hair is held up with a black velvet ribbon. She smiles and waves at him. He watches as she leads the couple towards his own parents. His heart sinks. Everyone will have to be introduced now.

'Father, Mother,' Huda says, 'I'd like you to meet Salah, my classmate and special friend.'

She is so enticing then, so strong and sure of herself that Salah knows he will not be going on that promised trip to faraway lands.

The first time Salah sees Aneesa she is waiting at the bus stop around the corner from the house. Her brown hair is frizzy and flies in the wind and she is dressed entirely in black with a pair of huge, bulky boots.

Salah sits beside her and is met with a breezy perfume of citrus fruits and jasmine. He cannot help staring at her profile. Her skin is luminous, he thinks, and that is what makes her beautiful.

The young woman suddenly turns to him and says hello but he is so surprised at the greeting that he cannot bring himself to say anything at first. Eventually, as they wait for a bus that is a long time in coming, they begin to talk and Salah feels his spirits lifting at the gentle rhythms in her words.

Living so intimately with a woman surprises him. Salah wonders if the experience of marriage for most men is like his own and is suddenly aware of a fastidiousness in himself that he had never known he possessed. Huda is as cautious as he is at first, tiptoeing around his emotions delicately, treating him with a deference she did not show when they were merely friends. Their love life consumes them in the first year of their marriage and he is happy with the secrecy of it, the fact that he can appear reserved and unperturbed to the outside world when his senses are reeling with thoughts of his young wife.

After a few weeks in his parents' home where the young couple enjoy limited privacy, they move to their own flat. Salah watches as Huda blossoms into something else, into a woman preoccupied with setting up a home and tending to it. They look for furniture together, going from shop to shop on Salah's days off and at the weekends, but Huda is the one who makes the decisions on what to buy and where to place it. Salah does not mind that his wife seems to have claimed everything domestic in their lives as her own. He notices also how, in subtle ways, she begins to push him out of her world, sometimes temporarily, sometimes indicating that this is a place to which he will never have access. I don't want you to worry about the housework and cooking, *habibi*, she says. Let me take care of that and you concentrate on your work. And to his surprise, he seems to love her more not less for this, as if in distancing herself from him she is introducing him to a more grown-up world where

116

responsibility comes before friendship and a more rigid idea of love before unruly passion.

In time, Salah comes to love their flat, its elegant style and pervading comforts, their streamlined bedroom and, especially, the enclosed balcony overlooking the sea from where he can ponder his fate. Yet he senses a nagging inside him, not quite a longing but a feeling that is less defined and more worrisome. Huda seems to have slipped away from him into a life of her own, into the mundane details of every day and the secret ambitions that she harbours for them as a couple, as though each no longer existed separately from the other. By the time he discovers what it is unsettling him, Salah cannot begin to imagine what to do about it and, anyway, Samir appears and their lives are tossed and turned and filled with joy and frustration and all the things between.

He likes to watch Huda bathe the baby, the way she slides her forearm under his tiny arms so he is held firmly up, above the water, as she gently cleans him with a flannel in her other hand. Salah stands there, fascinated but feeling useless, until Huda asks him to fetch the baby's towel and he can scoop his son up in his arms, wet, slithering, a breathing, living thing, a beating heart and the source of so much love. Salah is often left bereft when Huda eventually takes Samir away to dress him and make him ordinary again.

He is a quiet boy, though Salah cannot really tell since he has had no previous experience with young children and does not really remember being one himself. Perhaps, he sometimes thinks, it is because Samir is an only child. When he broaches the subject with Huda, asks her if it wouldn't be a good idea to have another, she bristles with annoyance and surprise. He is all I want in this world, she tells her husband, and Salah is effectively silenced, for what could he say then?

With time, Salah feels a gap between himself and his wife that is only remedied with Samir's presence, as if the child provided some kind of link between them, not in terms of being something to converse about and busy themselves with, but in being their common feeling, the place where their separate emotions touch and do not recoil. Although this truth worries Salah, makes him apprehensive about a future empty of connection, he does not see a way out and begins to wonder if his preoccupation with having another baby is only an attempt at stalling an inevitable decline.

He continues to hope, however, that his relationship with his son remains a substantial one, not necessarily strong but resilient and important, and he can see a time ahead when it will bring them both the comfort that they cannot now find in each other. He is affectionate with Samir in unobtrusive ways, as he watches him with tenderness at bedtime or when he passes a hand over the top of the boy's head, feeling a frisson at the touch of silky child hair, wanting to hold him but not daring to and envying his mother that she can do just that. In understanding that his upbringing has imposed this pretence at detachment, Salah does not attempt to upset or even circumvent it and is too afraid of the many things that will crumble around him if he does. It might be best, he tells himself, on nights when he cannot sleep and his wife's steady breathing does not comfort him, to let things be. It might be best now, he nods into the darkness, to yield.

* * *

Salah and Samir have just bought themselves a backgammon table from the Middle-Eastern shop where they do their weekend shopping. Samir does not know how to play very well but Salah has promised to teach him the intricacies of the game. They place the backgammon board on the kitchen table and sit at either side of it.

'I'll take black,' Samir says, and Salah nods.

'Do you know *mahbouseh*?' he asks his son.

'What's the difference?'

'*Mahbouseh* is the one where you can block your opponent's pieces . . .'

'That's the one I know!' Samir grins.

They set the stones on the backgammon table and each throws the dice to decide who will go first.

The stones, which are also made of wood, make a great deal of noise as the two men slam them down on the board.

'You're making mistakes, *habibi*,' Salah tells Samir, pointing to the stone his son has just moved. 'Put that one back and move the other one.'

Samir shakes his head.

'You're just trying to distract me, *baba*. Worry about your own game.' Moments later, Samir looks up at his father.

'Two out of three?' he asks.

'I'll only beat you again, Samir. Let's take a break and have something to drink.'

Salah goes to the kitchen worktop where they have placed their shopping and removes a bottle containing a dark liquid out of one of the plastic bags. He fetches two glasses and returns to the table.

'What is that?' Samir asks as Salah pours the drink into the glasses.

'*Jillab*. It's made from dates. Haven't you ever had it before?'

Samir takes a glass from his father and sips slowly at it.

'This is wonderful.'

'Strictly speaking, I should have put some pine nuts into the glass. They're great with it.'

Samir puts his glass down.

'I remember now,' he says softly.

Salah looks at his son.

'I remember going downtown with Mother when I was very young. There was a man who had a stall at the centre of the *souq* and he sold this. The stall was made of glass and coloured panels of wood.'

Salah nods.

'People would stop there for a drink. After they'd paid him, the man would take their glasses from them and rinse them under a tap that was on one side of his stall. I remember watching the water trickle down underneath people's feet but no one seemed to mind.'

Salah watches as his son wraps his hand around his empty glass and looks into the distance.

'I'd never seen anything like it, the noise, the crowds, the colour and the activity. It was like watching a stage show.' He looks back at Salah and smiles. 'When I asked Mother if I could have a glass of *jillab*, she said no. She said it was all very unsanitary or something.' He shakes his head and the sides of his mouth droop slightly. 'Can you imagine that, *baba*? Can you imagine that?'

*　　*　　*

There are some things that so completely define him that Salah cannot bring himself to speak of them to anyone. He knows, for instance, that were he to measure his life in terms of achievements, he would have to think of it as having been successful. He had carried out his duties to the letter and worked hard to provide for his wife and son, and his home had always been a refuge for family and friends. But he is equally certain of an unsteadiness in him that might have led him elsewhere, perhaps towards an exaggerated sense of pride, a misplaced confidence in his own importance.

As a young man, he had taken pleasure in the beauty of his body, its strength and agility and the ease with which he could satisfy its needs, so that when he chose his wife, desire as well as love had been the impetus. Now, if he allows his mind to wander away from what is undeniable – his love for the departed Huda and for Samir, and the dark fears that he has no wish to explore – if he ventures into the mysteries of his life, what he feels is a kind of physical wonder that begins in the pit of his stomach and makes his hands tremble with excitement.

I am old, Salah repeats to himself. Here are my creaking limbs, the bend and brittleness of my back. Still, something in him remains unconvinced, something tough and unrelenting. It is perhaps, he thinks to himself, the only thing in me that is still unpredictable and defiant. And of this he cannot help but feel a little proud.

When Samir takes his baccalaureate exam at eighteen, Salah discovers that Huda has made all the necessary preparations for their son to study abroad. She is adamant when Salah tries to discuss the subject with her.

'He's going to Europe, Salah,' Huda says. 'It's not the end of the world. He'll be better off there.'

'But with his grades he could easily get into the American University here. He'd get an excellent education there.'

'Just like you and I did, you mean?'

Salah feels his heart jump in his chest.

'What is the matter, Huda? What are you talking about?'

She turns away from him and busies herself with something on the desk. She does this only when she is trying to avoid his eyes.

'Well, we haven't done particularly well, have we? We're comfortable, I know, but we're not likely to get much further than this, you know that.'

Salah has worked for the same construction firm as a civil engineer ever since his graduation.

'You want him to be rich, is that it?' he objects. 'What I have given him is not enough?'

Huda turns around and looks straight at him.

'It's not just a question of money. He must be comfortable, of course, but I want more for him than that. I want him to get out of this country and see more of the world, be a part of the world. Besides, the political situation here is getting more precarious by the day. He's better off far away.'

Huda's eyes, which have always fascinated Salah because of their ability to change colour and reflect her mood, burn bright and green. He gets up from his seat, feeling a sudden but certain defeat. Who am I to put obstacles in the way of opportunities for my own son, he asks himself. Perhaps he will be better off away from us and away from Beirut. Looking out of an open window on the enclosed balcony, Huda no longer in his sight, Salah shakes his head and sniffs at the damp air. Although he has been able to swim ever since Huda taught him how all those years ago, he has not been to the beach in a long time. The sea is an undulating dark blue and to his eyes at least appears endless.

Aneesa tells him about her brother not long after Salah meets her. He feels he is beginning to understand her better, the sadness that seems always to be hovering around her eyes. And while he is certain that Bassam will have been murdered by his abductors – Salah lived long enough in the thick of the war to know that much – he cannot bring himself to say it to her. He believes that in some ways losing his wife to a terrible illness is somehow easier to bear for he cannot begin to imagine what it is like to know that someone you love endured unspeakable cruelty before dying.

'My mother continues to hope, though,' Aneesa says with a shrug of her shoulders. 'I try to discourage her from this when we talk on the phone but then I think it might be the wrong thing to do.' She looks at him as if to ask what he thinks but Salah says nothing. 'Maybe hope is the only thing she has now.'

But she has you, Salah begins to say and stops himself. Has she forgotten that she has you?

*   *   *

123

The civil war is unexpected. Salah wonders how he could have been so unaware of what was going on in his own country that he did not recognize the warning signals that had been apparent for a number of years. He is no longer averse to his son's leaving and is glad that he can afford to send him away from the inevitable carnage that will follow.

Once Samir goes away to university, Huda seems to have more time for Salah, although he is not certain if he is happy about the extra attention or simply feeling more constrained. On days when the fighting is at a minimum and it is safe to venture outside the apartment, they do things together as they had once done, dinners and outings and walks along the Corniche. Friends they have long neglected suddenly become a part of their lives again so that Salah feels he must relearn things he has forgotten over the years, how to make conversation and how to appear well read and cultured. But he is conscious of a need to maintain warm relationships at a time when so much hatred seems to have gripped the country and is glad that Huda is there to help him along. He is also aware that in maintaining these friendships, he and Huda, like so many of their circle in Beirut, are keeping certain aspects of the war at bay, the devastation and harshness that they will likely avoid until the moment arrives when it directly touches them. But he is astute enough to understand that while he plays no part in the sectarian divide that is tearing the country apart, by closing himself off from it he is doing nothing to push the hatred away. And through all this Salah feels Samir's absence, an empty seat at a dinner table brimming with food and people, an absent conversation about nothing in particular, the ghost of a presence in the flat. But he does not mention his fears to Huda, does not tell her that perhaps they no longer have anything real to share, that in leaving at so young an age, their son might never find the will to return. Instead, Salah attends to Huda and her feelings with the tenderness reserved for those one pities, not realizing that one day in the future compassion will be all he feels for his ailing wife.

Salah and Aneesa are having a picnic lunch on a park bench. It is sunny and warm and a large group of children in the playground close by are making a lot of friendly noise. Salah bites into his sandwich and peers closely at Aneesa. She is looking happy and beautiful, her cheeks turning pink in the sun and her hair shining.

'Will you have children of your own, do you think?' Salah asks her once he has finished chewing.

'Do you think I should?'

Salah turns to look at the playground and laughs.

'It would be like nothing else you have ever done.'

When Samir was born, a tiny bundle of dark hair and tears, Salah had thought him a stranger at first. But it was not long before, through holding him and watching him awake and asleep, Salah began to feel something between them, a connection that could only grow stronger, his heart claimed and kept for ever.

Aneesa gathers the sandwich wrapping and their napkins and gets up to throw them away. When she returns, Salah takes a thermos out of the plastic bag beside him and pours coffee into two plastic cups.

'Here you go, *habibti*,' he says, handing Aneesa one of the cups and taking the other for himself.

'You always make the best coffee, Salah.'

'The secret is in the beans. I get them from that Middle-Eastern bakery by the house. They're freshly roasted and I only ever grind them just before making the coffee.'

'Mmmm.'

The two sit happily sipping their coffee and watching the children in the playground. Some of them are playing in the sand pit, others are on the swings and on the climbing frame. They move from one to the other with seamless purpose, the transition from one activity to another, from one feeling to another, effortless and true. Aneesa leans forward on the bench beside Salah, resting her elbows on her knees. She has to lift her head up to see the playground and then bend it forward again to drink her coffee. He loves this naturalness about her and the ease she feels in his presence. When she sits up again, Salah takes the empty cup from her and places it along with his own in the plastic bag with the thermos. They both stand up, Aneesa stamping her feet on the ground and Salah looking back at the bench to make sure they have not left anything behind, and in that moment it comes to him. I am in love with all this, he thinks to himself with astonishment.

'They are lovely, aren't they?' Aneesa says, pointing to the playground.

Salah looks at her and nods.

He is beginning to feel the cold, a chill that goes through his clothes and penetrates his skin until it reaches his bones. You'll have to get used to this kind of weather, *baba*, Samir says to him as he opens windows upstairs and downstairs early every morning so that the house feels more like outside than in.

But Salah shuts all the windows again as soon as his son leaves for work, turning on the central heating and putting the kettle on for a warming cup of sugary tea. It's unnatural, he mutters to himself, to laugh at the elements like this.

He remembers Huda bundling Samir up in the winter. I don't want him to catch cold, she would say, zipping up the child's jacket, wrapping a scarf around his neck and pulling a woollen hat over his head. He had marvelled at how still Samir could be when his mother was fussing over him.

Let's go, son. Let's go and find the snow in the mountains, Salah would say as he led his son out of the front door. Then there was Samir, up on a hill, standing next to a snowman whose uneven head tilts dangerously to one side, his coat and scarf on the snow beside him, his cheeks red and his hair plastered to his small head, a sight to see.

Huda's body is blistering with pain and Salah is no longer certain he has the strength to cope with it. The doctors at the hospital tell him to take her home, to find a nurse who will administer the necessary medications and wait for the end to come. When he telephones Samir he tells him not to come for a week or two.

'She would not want you to see her like this, *habibi*. Wait until she has settled down a bit and she is able to talk to you.'

But the day when Huda settles into her misery does

not come. She passes away in the night, with Salah at her side and a promise that Samir will never know how bad things had been for her at the end.

Not long after the funeral, on a quiet afternoon when Huda's absence makes it impossible for him to stay in the flat, Salah dresses carefully and goes down the stairs to the art gallery on the floor below. He had read a notice in the lift only the day before of a new exhibition and he decides he might as well go and see it.

The paintings are mostly modern, splashes of colour on huge canvases that make him think of loud, discordant music. He wanders around the rooms of the gallery during the opening, a drink in hand, and looks tentatively at the artwork, straining to hear the conversations around him.

As he stands leafing through the brochure he was handed at the door, Salah looks up to find the gallery owner beside him.

'What do you think?' she asks.

Salah feels suddenly nervous.

'Very nice. I was just reading up on the artist.'

The woman puts a hand on his arm and leans closer towards him.

'You're our neighbour from upstairs, aren't you?' She smiles at him. 'I imagine this sort of thing isn't much to your taste.'

He shakes his head.

'Why don't you come with me into the office? I have a painting I want to show you that I'm certain you'd like.'

Once inside, the woman lifts a painting from a stack leaning against the wall on to a large desk.

'It's by a Greek artist. I had wanted to keep it for myself.'

Salah looks closely at the seeming chaos of colours until they make sense to him.

'It's an angel, isn't it?'

He touches it through the glass with the tips of his fingers. When he finally lifts his head, he sees the gallery owner smiling at him and suddenly realizes where he is now and where his thoughts have been.

When Samir comes to Beirut following Huda's death, he suggests that his father return with him to London. But Salah is unprepared. He will have to speak more openly to his son, he knows. As it is, they meet each morning as if for the first time, inching their way through reluctant conversations, only warming up to each other in their thoughts and after they have parted.

Salah begins by bringing Huda up at odd moments or by suddenly mentioning her after long periods of silence between them.

'Do you remember when she used to bring you to my office after school?' he would say and then wait for Samir to nod in agreement. 'Everyone admired her there, you know.'

One day, he grabs on to his son's arm as they walk and bends his head low to his ear.

'She never asked me for money, you know that?' Salah begins. 'I used to urge her to reach into my pocket and take out whatever she wanted but she always refused.' He realizes there is a note of despair in his voice. 'I gave her enough for household expenses and some extra to spend on herself but she used to save whatever was left

129

over. For Samir, she told me later when I found out about it. For his future.'

They walk a few moments longer in silence.

'Did you know, son?' Salah finally asks. 'Did you realize then just how much your mother loved you?'

When Samir arrives to take him away, Salah is unprepared. He tries to dissuade Samir of the notion of departure, even suggests that his son should return to Beirut to live but Samir is adamant. Salah recognizes the same underlying scorn for the country that Huda used to feel and is saddened for his son's sake that there should be no place for which he harbours unquestioning love.

Before they leave, Salah slowly goes through the flat, trying to decide what he will take with him. He packs a suitcase of his own clothes and begins to fill another but Samir tells him to leave many things behind as they will buy new things once they get to London. Just take the bare necessities, *baba*, he tells him, and we'll get the rest over there. It's much better quality anyway. Then Salah wonders if he should take something of Huda's as a keepsake to remember her by, but eventually decides against it since she is always in his thoughts anyway. Samir tells him they cannot take any furniture with them – We are not leaving the flat for ever, *baba*, we'll be back again – so Salah tears up some old bed sheets and places them on the sofas and chairs against the inevitable dust of time.

Just as he is about to end his search, Salah comes upon the painting. It is not the only one in the flat nor is it the most valuable but he does not question his desire to take it along. He looks at the bold strokes of colour, seemingly random but together forming one certain image. The gallery owner had told him that different people saw different things in it but Salah cannot understand how. He shows it to Samir and waits for his son to comment. Very nice, Samir says. We'll wrap it up carefully and take it with us if you like. But what do you see in it, Salah insists, pointing to the angel, to the tip of its wings and the glow of colour above its head. Samir shakes his head and smiles. It's an angel, of course. Is that what you've come to at your age, *baba*? Is it angels that you believe in now?

Samir and his father drive to Aneesa's block of flats to pick her up for dinner.

'I could have met you there,' Aneesa protests as she gets into the car.

Salah notices that her smile is a little nervous. She has on a long black dress with a wine-coloured shawl wrapped around her shoulders. She is also wearing a pair of drop earrings and has put on some make-up.

When they arrive at the restaurant, Salah pulls out a chair for Aneesa before he sits down.

'Thank you,' she says, looking at him, and in that instant, in the turn of her face, her soft cheek as it dips forward in gratitude and the unexpected colour in her lips, he realizes he has just had a glimpse of the woman in her.

Salah is wearing a suit for the occasion and had advised Samir to do the same, though unlike Samir he does not take his jacket off but chooses, instead, to keep it on, lifting his arms slightly to pull back the sleeves just before he picks up his knife and fork.

'My father tells me you're a translator.' Samir looks at Aneesa as he speaks.

'Yes, I translate documents for government departments.'

Salah watches Aneesa pick at her food, her shawl slipping off her shoulders and falling into the bend of her elbows.

'Do you enjoy your work?' Samir continues.

When Aneesa says nothing, he pushes his tie up against his neck and grunts.

'Shall we have more wine?' Samir asks before gesturing to the waiter to come to their table.

Salah looks at Aneesa. Her lipstick has faded on to the outer edges of her lips and she has one hand held up to her face. He reaches out and touches her arm.

'You look beautiful tonight, my dear,' Salah says softly. 'Did I neglect to tell you that?'

Salah and Samir go for a drive in the country one Saturday, to a village where the houses are small and quaint and greenery is everywhere. The day is somewhat cloudy and threatens rain but they have time before the storm to take a walk up into the hills that overlook the village and contemplate the beauty of a patchwork of open fields.

Standing there, Salah realizes how vast the world is and how circumspect his own life has been. He thinks that if he were young again he would do a few things differently; he would travel, perhaps, or simply let himself be. He no longer understands why it was always so important to have a purpose that drove him and wishes he had occasionally succumbed to his innate sense of adventure and drawn his wife and child into it also.

Perhaps if I had loved Huda more, he ponders. Perhaps then things would have turned out differently.

He lets out a long sigh and feels Samir come up behind him. His son puts an arm around his shoulders and Salah turns to look at him They gaze at each other for a long moment before making their way back down the hill to the village pub where they will have their lunch. As they descend, Samir walking ahead and turning every few moments to guide his father, Salah senses that a measure of closeness has been restored between them.

The airport café is crowded. Salah and Aneesa push their chairs closer to their table to let a couple with a trolley loaded with luggage go past. The coffee in their cups pitches forward and spills on to the saucers. Salah steadies the table and pushes the napkin holder towards Aneesa.

'Here we go,' Aneesa says as she places a napkin under each of their cups.

'Did you get anything on your clothes?'

She looks down at her shirt and trousers and shakes her head.

'No.'

'You want to arrive looking your best.'

Aneesa laughs nervously.

'I shall miss you,' she says.

Salah puts one hand, palm down, on the table and taps it with the other.

'And I shall miss seeing you do that,' Aneesa says. 'You always cup one hand and pat the other with it when you've got something on your mind.'

Salah looks down at the table before speaking.

133

'I never realized.'

Aneesa's smile falters.

'I know.'

For a moment, they are enveloped by the noise around them: overhead announcements; the sound of luggage being wheeled back and forth across the terminal floor; people's voices and nondescript music interlaced in the background. Salah closes his eyes and feels the artificial light penetrate through his thin lids. When he opens them again, Aneesa is looking at him.

'They did a good job packaging the painting,' he says. 'It'll be fine in the luggage compartment.'

Aneesa nods. She is grasping her handbag close to her body.

Salah holds a hand to his mouth and coughs.

'I think I'd better go in now,' Aneesa says.

They stand up slowly. Salah notices that there are two people, cups in hand, waiting to sit at their table. He leads Aneesa out of the café and stands with her at the entrance to the departure lounge. He places his hand on her arm.

'I shall miss you, my dear,' he says. 'It will not be the same without you here.'

Aneesa begins to cry.

'I'll see you again soon,' she says, sniffing loudly. 'You'll come back to Beirut, I know.'

He bends down, puts his arms around her and kisses her on the cheek and then leads her gently towards the queue going into the departure lounge.

'Hurry up now, Aneesa,' Salah says and then watches her turn and walk away.

*   *   *

Salah hates the shuffling most of all, the sound of his slippered feet as he moves across the marble floors in the kitchen, up the stairs and along the magnificent Persian carpet that covers his bedroom floor. At night, when he cannot sleep, preferring instead to stand listening to his loneliness as it whispers through the kitchen window – the light from the refrigerator left open faint and strangely comforting – he thinks on the life and times he once had. Of Samir as a young boy shimmying up a pine tree, monkey-like, his denims scraping against the scales of the narrow trunk, making them break off and fly upwards, his small feet crossed and meeting in front in one great hug. Of Huda, during those final days when her eyes began to fail, laying her two hands on his face, tracing his features with tremulous fingers and stirring in him thoughts of dizzying, youthful desires before her joy suddenly turned into rasping coughs and he, despite the nearly overwhelming sorrow that enveloped him, feeling an inexplicable disappointment. Of Aneesa, holding his hand as they stand at a bus stop, her unkempt hair flying in the wind and his heart stopping at the sight.

Some days, when Samir comes home from work and finds him sitting on a stool by the island in the centre of the kitchen, stirring a cup of steaming tea, the sugar bowl beside him, his pyjama top askew and his thin ankles visible above the leather slippers Huda had bought him years ago, Salah hears his son sigh with frustration as he turns on the light and reaches out to him, whispering words of comfort, shaking his head and leading him upstairs, and Salah wanting all the time to tell him, If only you knew, my son. If only you knew.

PART FIVE

S amir is sitting on the enclosed balcony of the flat
where he grew up. The windows are open wide and
the breeze makes the dust on all the surfaces – wicker
chairs, glass table and tiled floor – whirl around in the
fading sunlight. The sound of traffic from the street below
drifts up and turns into a comforting hum.

This is the first time I have ever been entirely on my
own here, he thinks to himself. What do I do now?

He shifts in his seat. The smells of Beirut never change:
pungent like the Mediterranean, slightly damp and
dusty. They are as familiar to him as the scent of his
own skin.

He gets up slowly and walks to the edge of the balcony
to look out at the sea. It is the beginning of autumn but
the water is still a deep blue and the sun, as it sets, shim-
mers a rich, warm red. A handful of people are walking
on the Corniche across the road but everything – the
sounds and the sights of home – appears muffled to him.

He feels the impulse to lift up his arms in triumph, but they remain pinned to his side.

When Salah died, Samir had felt exactly like this, dejected and unable to understand how anything so mysterious could have happened to him. Only yesterday, it seemed, his father had been lying in his bed, Samir smoothing back his hair and whispering comforting words to him.

He walks back inside the flat and begins to turn lights on but the rooms remain dark, their dim corners now engulfed in the shadows created by the light. He carries his suitcases into his parents' bedroom, pulls back the curtains and opens the windows but does not look out.

I will just have to spend my first night smothered in despair, Samir says out loud. He lies down on the bed and closes his eyes.

Ever since Salah's stroke, Samir has approached the task of taking care of his father methodically, running through every step in his mind before beginning, and then carrying everything out gently, though without hesitation.

Salah is no longer the same man. The right side of his face droops so that an involuntary tear often drips through his half-open eye and down his cheek, going unnoticed until Samir, tissue at the ready, leans towards him to wipe it off. He can no longer walk unaided and his speech, once precise and beautifully delivered, has become slurred, words running into each other, sputtering through the side of his mouth, hopeless and unintelligible. His right hand remains curled inwards into an uneven ball that has to be prised open, the long, tapered fingers unfurling with difficulty like trembling petals then falling in upon themselves as soon as Salah lets his guard down.

Samir pours shampoo over his father's head.

'Close your eyes,' he says loudly, over the sound of the water.

Salah's hair is still thick and mats easily. Samir rubs his scalp gently in a circular motion until he has created a generous lather.

'OK, *baba*, I'm going to rinse now. Keep your eyes shut . . . Is the water all right, *baba*?' Samir continues. 'Not too hot?'

Salah shakes his head, his eyes still tightly shut, his face screwed up as if with distaste. After turning the shower off, Samir hands his father a towel and goes back into the bedroom to fetch clean underwear and a fresh pair of pyjamas. He returns to the bathroom, helps Salah out of the shower cubicle and on to the walker where he dries him thoroughly and rubs moisturizing cream over his body before helping him to dress.

'This will stop your skin from getting too itchy,' he says, gesturing to the tube of lotion.

Salah's arms suddenly begin to tremble. Samir quickly puts the toilet lid down and sits his father down on it.

'Please,' says Salah, reaching out for his son's trousers and pulling on them.

'Yes, *baba*. What is it?'

Salah presses his lips together and points at the bathroom cabinet. Samir opens the cabinet and points at the different objects inside: his own toothpaste and some aftershave.

'Your cologne is in the bedroom,' Samir says. 'I'll go and get it.'

'No!' Salah's voice is surprisingly loud. He puts his hands on either side of the walker and lifts himself up again. He moves forward, towards the cabinet, and reaches for the toothpaste but it tumbles off the shelf and falls into the sink. Samir suddenly feels overcome with hopelessness.

'Do you want to brush your teeth?' he asks.

Salah nods.

'I haven't been doing that for you, *baba*. I'm sorry . . . I didn't think.'

Salah leans over the walker, his shoulders drooping with his weight, and lifts his head to look at his son.

'I'll get a new toothbrush from my room,' Samir says, rushing out.

Salah holds on to the basin and Samir stands beside him with the toothbrush. Salah opens his mouth while his son gingerly brushes his teeth. Salah's gums bleed slightly at the touch of the toothbrush. Then Samir turns on the tap, gathers water in his cupped hand and lifts it to the older man's mouth. Salah bends down so that Samir can see the back of his neck, thin and taut, and spits into the basin. When they are done, Samir pats his father's mouth dry with a face cloth.

'Does that feel better?' Samir asks, watching his father's face in the mirror.

Salah reaches for the toothbrush and places it on the side of the basin. He taps the surface of the basin with one hand and totters dangerously to one side so that Samir has to grab him to stop him from falling. Then they walk slowly out of the bathroom, Samir thinking back on the once deliberate beauty of his father's movements, the ebb and flow of his hands.

*　　　*　　　*

Samir misses being with a woman, the feel of her and the smell too. He is certain that love in this tired bed of lost passions would bring life back to him and fill up the silent spaces in the flat. He is astonished that he should continue to think of himself as an outsider in a place where there is no one left to make him feel like one, and wishes he had the strength in him to fight back. In returning to Beirut he has recalled a measure of himself, that place where he is at his most vulnerable, where living is not merely a recollection but a breathing, sorrowful thing. There had been no alternative to coming back, not once Salah had died and all Samir had been left with was this heaving sense of loss. He realizes how much he misses his father, not just his presence – which at times was persistent and perplexing – but his unspoken thoughts and the life he had kept so closely to himself, the loves he had cherished. Perhaps, he thinks, I will find here what my father was so anxious for me to find.

Samir remembers the first time he came back to Beirut after his mother's death and tried to persuade his father to leave with him. Salah had refused. Why don't you stay here, son, Salah had said. We don't belong in the West. This is our home.

Several days later, Samir and his father were on their way to the airport in a taxi; Salah was very quiet. I'm alone too now, *baba*, Samir had pleaded, tapping his father on the arm. I need you with me.

Now, the morning after his arrival, Samir wanders listlessly through the flat. He goes into the kitchen and begins to open cupboard doors. He takes out cleaning liquid, a bucket and a mop, a duster and a broom with a straw handle and feathery bristles. He bends down and passes the broom over the floor, back and forth and with a regular rhythm. The dirt lifts and falls. He fills the bucket with water, adds soap and throws the mop in as well. He remembers to look for rubber gloves and finds them in the cupboard under the sink. They are yellow and dry and begin to fall to pieces when he tries to put them on. With his bare hands, he takes the mop out of the bucket, squeezes the excess water out and begins to clean the kitchen floor.

Throughout the day, Samir finds himself wanting to stop but something makes him go on, an urgency that he cannot quite understand. By the early evening, his parents' bedroom, where he is now sleeping, the bathroom, the kitchen and the balcony are spotless. Samir has even taken out the few pieces of china and cutlery that his father had used just before he left and cleaned them for his own use. He is tired but suddenly very happy.

I'm hungry, Samir realizes.

He puts on a light jacket and goes out to look for something to eat.

My father, Samir daydreams as he stands swaying in the crowded underground train. My father should outlive me. He is everything a man should be, strong and kind and given to outbursts of dazzling anger.

He raps the knuckles of his right hand on his forehead and shakes his head. He is going in to work for the last time and feels exhilarated at the thought of starting all over again, of taking care of Salah and living within the details of everyday life, being a part of it in ways he had never managed before.

'Aha!' Samir says out loud and watches as the woman next to him scuttles to the other end of the carriage.

He remembers leaning over a balcony railing as a child to stare at the moving patterns made by the sunlight on the wall beneath. His head had begun to get heavy when he felt two large hands pull him up by the shoulders.

'Allah, Samir,' Salah says, pushing him gently towards the door that leads into the living room. 'Do you imagine you can fly? Don't let your mother see you doing that.'

As the train comes to a stop at his station, Samir pulls his fingers further into his leather gloves and trips over his feet while stepping out into the throng.

He has always resembled his mother, her compact body and the way she moved through life with purpose. Even at night, as she tucked him into bed, whispering goodnight and I love you into his ear, she did it, he knew, with a view of the task ahead, tending to Salah perhaps or making plans for the next day's chores.

Samir has grown into the same urgency, a kind of singular impatience to complete what cannot be completed, approaching everything as a challenge that would only lead to yet another and soon feeling weariness tapping at his skin and seeping into his body, until all he can do is to rub his hand hard back and forth across his chest to shift the pain.

Yet with his father, Samir has known a halting friendship, the kind of closeness that could weather constant interruption. He is aware of an urgent need to tend to Salah. He sees no reason to differentiate between their new roles, to recognize one as giver and the other as recipient. Compassion, Samir has only recently come to understand, courses through and beyond the confines of our own selves on its endless journey through our hearts.

At this stage, Samir still has a window of opportunity. The headaches always begin with a tingling in his fingers and a vagueness to his thoughts that makes everything he sees appear filmy and unfocused. There is a moment during which he can take medication and then hope, quietly, that it will work. The first sign of the tablets working is when the sensation in his fingers starts to fade away; only then does he begin to think he has success-fully avoided jumping over the precipice once again, as if he had just been given a second chance.

But when the medicine proves ineffective, when he starts to wish he hadn't waited so long before taking it, when there is nothing to save him from the nausea and the retching and the agony except time, he resigns himself to the pain, draws the curtains and lies back on the bed wanting only to die.

And when it's all over, when he can sit up and breathe easily again, a wave of something bigger than relief, some-thing like grace, sweeps over him and he is suddenly, in-explicably, overwhelmed with gratitude.

When the headaches first started, Samir had been a teenager. He remembers the feel of his mother's palm on his forehead, cooling even in the throes of fire. She would wet a small towel with cold water from the kitchen tap and then place it on his face and head before kneading his hands with it, pulling at his fingers slightly so that he felt the tension in them ease a little. And as soon as he lifted his head, almost overcome with queasiness, she would walk him to the bathroom and stand over him as he was sick.

'Here, *habibi*. Have a glass of water. Rinse your mouth out now.'

Then back in his dark bedroom, his father hovering nervously in the doorway, Huda would tuck Samir into the bed, expertly and with the same precision she had used when he was a very young child.

'There now, you'll feel better after that, Samir,' she would say. 'Don't worry now, darling, they're just the same silly headaches I used to get when I was your age. They'll eventually go away. You know they're a sign of a sensitive nature.'

But the threat of pain remains with him now. He only gets the headaches once or twice a year at the most but that is often enough to keep him on his toes, to push him into a kind of gentle acquiescence, into admitting a vulnerability that he does not wish to acknowledge. Yes, I have rather a delicate system, he tells himself and others who care to know, yes, I do have to be careful but it's all right really, I'll be fine.

The house stands on the outer edge of a park on a road that bends slightly inwards, enclosing the pavement and the buildings that line the street in a gentle arch of trees and neat green.

Salah's bed has been moved into what used to be the library, on the ground floor of the house, and is placed directly beneath a large window that looks out on to the view. Samir spends several hours of the day in an armchair next to his father's bed reading or simply staring out of the window. Cars regularly drive down the road and pedestrians walk past on the winding pavement, both too far away to be heard but close enough to be seen and observed.

'Do you see the woman with the baby, *baba*? She's about to cross the road and go into the park.'

The two men watch the figure pushing the pram. She has her back to them and stops for a moment to bend down towards the baby. Once in the park, she disappears down a path beyond the trees and their gaze.

Samir turns his attention back to his father. Salah is trying to straighten the small cotton blanket placed on top of the duvet and over his legs. The three outer fingers on his right hand are bent inwards and he is unable to grip the blanket firmly. Samir takes his father's hand in both of his own and attempts, gently, to straighten his fingers.

'It is good to be here together, isn't it, *baba*?'

But when he looks at Salah's face, he is unable to read it. There is firmness around the lips, as though they have been pushed together with disapproval, but Salah's eyes, appearing small now under the folds of his eyelids, are alert and questioning.

'Do you need anything, *habibi*? Can I get you anything?'

Salah lies back against the pillows, smacks his lips together and looks out towards the park once again.

Samir walks on the other side of the Corniche, where the fast-food places are and the ice cream and sweet shops. It is busy and there are people, families and groups of young men, wandering up and down the street. Men push carts carrying sweets and nuts and ears of corn cooked over hot coal up and down the Corniche and children on bicycles weave their way around them. The cars on the road drive up dangerously close to the pavement, come to a sudden stop and then park at impossible angles or alongside other vehicles before their passengers step out slamming doors and talking loudly. It is the kind of chaotic, teeming noise that Samir has not heard in a while and it makes him aware of something in himself that he has long ignored.

He goes into a fish-and-chip shop, orders and takes his food and drink to an outside table. The fish is battered and crumbly and the potatoes are crispy. As he sips at his drink, he notices a woman with short grey hair and a young boy sitting at a table not too far from his own. They are talking animatedly as they eat, their chairs and their heads close together. They are both in jeans and trainers, though she is wearing a white top and he is in a blue shirt. The woman says something and the boy puts his head back and laughs out loud. Samir reaches for his soft drink and when he looks up again, the woman is gazing at him. She raises her hand and waves. Samir feels himself stiffen and only relaxes when she finally turns away. In any event, he thinks, I would not know what to say.

He takes a circuitous route home, away from the Corniche and on to the parallel street. Many new buildings have gone up since he was last here. There are small hotels and blocks of furnished flats with neon signs on the outside and doormen in uniform. Garages where dozens of vehicles crowd against each other and spill out on to the pavement alternate with clothing and other shops on one side of the street. These are changes that, strangely enough, appeal to him, that make the neighbourhood appear less staid than it did when he was a child.

He has on soft shoes and though the pavements are uneven, with cars parked across them so hc has to walk on the street most of the time, he feels himself glide effortlessly across the ground. It is a lightness of being that he has not felt for a long time. I am tied to nothing, Samir thinks to himself. Watch me fly, *baba*.

Salah takes on the housekeeping very soon after his arrival. Samir is at first amused by his father's sudden interest in everything domestic and eventually feels something close to admiration for Salah's newly acquired skills at keeping the house in order.

'I never knew you cared about such things,' Samir tells him one day. 'Mother said you were hopeless at it.'

'That's because she never let me anywhere near the kitchen,' Salah replies with a shrug of his shoulders, 'or the cupboards and the cleaning things. I always assumed she was right.'

He is loading the dishwasher with the same unconscious grace as he does everything else, Samir thinks as he watches his father. He begins by scraping the plates empty and rinsing them along with mugs and cutlery thoroughly under the tap. Then he bends down carefully to place them neatly on the racks. He is a pleasure to watch, Samir thinks.

'But we already have someone to clean the place, *baba*,' Samir eventually says. 'I don't want you to tire yourself out.'

'There's a lot more to keeping house than just cleaning, *habibi*.'

Salah puts the soap powder in its compartment, shuts the door of the dishwasher and turns it on. Then he straightens up, taps the kitchen worktop with the fingers of one hand and turns around with a look of great satisfaction on his face.

Thoughts of his childhood come regularly into Samir's mind and sometimes when he least expects them, as he sits in the kitchen folding the laundry or while looking out at the view from the flat's balcony. He suddenly sees himself, small and neatly dressed, walking alongside his mother on a Beirut street, his hand resting on her handbag; or standing in the doorway of his parents' bedroom watching her as she applies her make-up. There is something about the way the boy carries himself, seemingly self-contained, almost defiant, and in the way he looks at his mother, his eyes questioning her every move.

But there are things he does not need to recall for they have stayed with him through adulthood, such as the silence that always pervaded the rooms of the flat, following his parents around so closely that they seemed outlined by it, a kind of glow that encompassed him as well, though it disappeared as soon they stepped outside and into the beckoning world. His aloneness also, not the self-pity sometimes associated with loneliness, but a kind of impatience with things outside his immediate circle, with those who would be friends and events that did not directly affect him.

As an adult, Samir realizes, he has been less than forthcoming, has hidden a measure of arrogance beneath what others sometimes see as mere reticence. It gives him the sense that in everything he feels, even now with the sorrow over the loss of his father, lies a measure of falseness, so that he is often compelled to say, Don't pay any attention, please, it's just me pretending again, though he does not know who he might say this to.

Now, discovering this humbler, less-assured version of himself settling into Beirut as though it had never belonged anywhere else, Samir wonders what might come next. He is astonished also that this flat which, in his parents' lifetime, had held so much fascination for him, both good sensations and others that were indifferent, has suddenly lost its associations. This, after all, could be any kitchen, he mutters to himself, and these rooms are like many others I have been in. I, Samir concludes as he stands rigid in the centre of the hushed living room, could be anywhere in this wide world.

He walks into the house one evening and finds Salah and a young woman sitting on the Persian carpet in the living room. The coffee table has been pushed to one side and they have their backs against the sofa, with their legs stretched out towards the fireplace. They are both shoeless, Salah in his grey silk socks, and the woman in black matt tights that have a slight run at one heel. They stand up to greet him when he comes in.

'Hello, I'm Aneesa,' the young woman says.

Her brown hair forms a frizzy halo that frames an already round face and she is wearing a knee-length corduroy dress in an unbecoming shade of purple with a denim jacket buttoned over it. She holds out her hand to him and smiles. He realizes she is the same young woman he saw as he was rushing out of the house weeks earlier. This time, he notices her skin, clear and so radiant it seems as if he has just lifted his head up to the sky and met the moonlight with his eyes.

'Hello.'

Samir looks at his father.

'We've already eaten, *habibi*,' says Salah, 'but I could heat something up for you.'

'It's all right, *baba*. I had dinner earlier.'

They stand, the three of them, by the fire. He can feel the heat of it on his legs. When he looks down, he sees that Aneesa's toes are curled inwards and Salah's long, thin feet are lined one against the other. His own black shoes, clumsy and awkward, shine in the firelight and complete the circle.

Samir has bought his father a wheelchair to take him out for walks in the park. The first time they go out, Salah asks to wear his suede jacket, the camel hair scarf that goes with it and the gloves that Aneesa gave him. Samir wraps a woollen throw around his father's legs just before they step outside the front door.

The cold is bearable, Samir thinks as he pushes the chair on to the pavement and prepares to go across the road. There aren't too many cars driving past but he nonetheless waits until the road is completely empty before going across it and then up the ramp that leads into the park.

'Not many leaves left on the trees, are there, *baba*? Still, it's nice to be out again, isn't it?'

It rained earlier in the day and the cement path is still dark and wet. Samir stops and bends down to pull Salah's scarf up around his ears. He looks into his father's eyes for a moment and smiles.

'You look like I used to when Mum wrapped me up

153

in all those clothes on our trips to the snow. Do you remember, *baba*?'

Salah nods and smiles weakly back at Samir. Then he points ahead and they begin to move again. Samir leans into the chair and pushes hard. Salah has lost a great deal of weight but the wheelchair is heavy. There are no children playing in the park because it is still relatively early in the morning. The two men go past the green field that footballers use as a pitch at weekends and over the stream and the small bridge leading to the other side of the park. Salah points again.

'Do you want to go and sit by the pond, *baba*?' Samir asks. 'It might be too cold but we'll try anyway.'

They move leisurely down to the water and when they get there Samir stops and puts on the wheelchair brakes.

'It's a beautiful view, isn't it, *baba*? Look at those geese over there. They've come all the way from Canada, you know. And there is a duck diving into the water.'

The pond is dark and still except where the birds are quietly moving across its surface and leaving a faint ripple of light behind them. A squirrel scampers up to the chair and sits up on its luxuriant tail.

Salah looks up at Samir and Samir nods with a smile. Salah hangs his head and frowns. He holds out his hand.

'Bread?'

'We didn't bring any bread with us, *baba*. Did you want to feed the animals?'

Salah continues to look at Samir.

'I'm sorry, *habibi*. I'll be sure to bring something for them next time we come. I didn't think of it.'

Salah turns his head away to look at the pond once again. Samir steps up behind him and places a hand on his father's shoulder. The park has turned suddenly quiet and Samir decides it is time to go back home.

His parents took him on trips to the mountains when he was a child. They would get into the car, Samir sitting up on his knees by the window in the back, and drive up winding roads, past hills covered in trees and bush. If he opened the window just a little and lifted his head towards it, Samir could feel the air that came through, changing and emptying him somehow, so that when he breathed it in it created a big hollow inside him that was impossible to fill.

As soon as they reached a village, Samir's father would slow the car down so that they could look at the houses, stone with red roofs, on either side of the street and further up in the hills.

'Look at that one, *habibi*,' his mother would say. 'Can you see it all the way up there? It's so well hidden behind the trees, isn't it?'

And Samir would strain to see what had fascinated her so much, feeling a familiar disappointment when it proved to be just another old house among the tall umbrella pines.

'Can we go get some water from the spring now?'

They would drive around looking for the spring that most mountain villages had and Salah would stop the car as soon as they found it, motioning to Samir to come out and help. In the trunk of the car, Samir would pull out the big blue plastic container with a red top and make his way down the stone steps of the spring with it.

'Don't worry, *baba*. I'll do it on my own. You don't need to come with me.'

He unscrewed the top and placed the container underneath the spout. The water came out in a constant stream and was somewhere between a trickle and a gush. What didn't go into the container poured into a stone bowl and down a drain at the side. He wondered where it went after that.

As the container filled up, the sound the water made going into it changed, echoing loudly and becoming deeper. Samir bent down, cupped a hand over the spout and brought it to his mouth. The water was cold and very good.

When the container was filled up, he screwed its cap back on, stood up and lifted it with both hands before making his way up the steps. It was very heavy and hung low close to his feet. Samir had to lift both his elbows up so he wouldn't trip over the container as he climbed up the steps again and past the people who were waiting their turn. His parents stood at the top of the steps watching him and, for a moment, Samir could almost hear them urging him on though they said nothing. He tripped and heard his mother's gasp. Then he straightened up and started up the steps again.

'Here you go, *baba*,' he said once he reached the top.

'Well done, *habibi*. I'll put the container in the back and you two get in. We've got a long way to go yet.'

Then they would go to have lunch in a restaurant in one of the larger towns in the area and on the drive home later in the afternoon, Samir would imagine he could hear the water sloshing back and forth in its container in the boot of the moving car.

*   *   *

It is autumn and the beaches, long and white, are deserted. Samir has made a trip to the south to visit the cities of Sidon and Tyre that his father had always loved. The sun appears reluctantly from behind clouds to warm the sand and here, surrounded by sea and verdant valleys, his heart lurching as he walks, Samir thinks of death: his mother's passing and Salah's sudden demise.

Where do they go, he wonders, those who die? It is impossible for him to think of anywhere that is not a place, and impossible too to imagine that those he had known so well could suddenly disappear.

When his mother died, he had not been there, had not seen her slowly weaken into something else, something not so strong or enduring, so that he has never quite been able to believe her absence. She appeared to Samir in a dream on the night his father told him of her death, not a shadow of the woman he had known, but an evanescent being that he instantly recognized as Huda before and after death. They sat together, Samir and his mother, in that quiet time between lives, and spoke of everything that had happened between them, without urgency and with complete acceptance. In reminding him of their life together, she had also intimated that he was everything she had ever wanted in a son. When Samir finally awoke early the next morning, he had felt almost happy with relief.

But with his father, Samir suddenly realizes, there had been no acknowledgement of parting and Salah has already slipped into a shapeless past, an essential part of the man Samir has become but elusive nonetheless.

He is surprised at the extent of his pleasure in the feeble sunlight. The sand makes his feet heavy as he walks and he has to bend forward with the effort. It is Sunday and he is in shorts and a T-shirt with a sweater over his shoulders. He stops and looks down at his legs, at the light covering of dark hair against white skin. I am fading too, he mutters, rubbing his hands roughly back and forth along his thighs before straightening up again. He wonders what it would be like to have someone with him, a woman, perhaps. He thinks of Aneesa again. She is dressed in a long shift dress and bare feet and is walking towards him across the sand, one hand up, waving, the setting sun behind her. The horizon stretches outwards before him, a grey-blue emptiness above a distant line of water. Samir nods in approval and moves on.

Aneesa has not yet arrived when Samir returns to the house from work.

'Are we sitting at the table in here?' he asks his father as he walks into the kitchen.

'I think it's friendlier, don't you?' Salah replies. 'Besides, Aneesa doesn't mind. She likes it in here.'

'I just thought that since we hardly ever use the dining room . . .'

'Exactly.' Salah turns away to stir something in a pot on the stove.

'All right, then,' Samir says after a pause and goes up to his room to change.

When he comes downstairs again, Aneesa is seated at the island in the middle of the kitchen. She does not stand up this time.

'Your father won't let me help,' she says, 'so I thought I'd just make myself comfortable.'

'I'll open a bottle of wine and join you,' says Samir.

'I'm no good at cooking so I'd better keep out of it.'

He hears himself speak as he takes out a bottle of red wine, opens it and fetches some glasses. His voice sounds distant in his head but she seems to be reacting appropriately to it, nodding, smiling and glancing towards Salah every now and then.

They sit down to eat, Salah at the head of the table and Aneesa and Samir on either side of him. Salah picks up a large spoon and serves them the roast chicken and potatoes.

'Help yourselves to the salad,' he says.

'What is that wonderful flavour?' Aneesa asks moments later.

'Rosemary. I marinated the chicken in garlic, herbs and lemon before putting it in the oven.'

'Rosemary,' Aneesa repeats. 'It translates as mountain laurel in Arabic.'

'*Ikleel al jabal*,' Salah says.

Aneesa smiles and goes back to her food.

Samir feels agitated at the ensuing silence. His knife slips from his hand and falls to the floor. He bends down to pick it up.

'Excuse me,' he says as he gets up and places it in the kitchen sink. He takes another knife out of the cutlery drawer and stops before returning to the table.

Salah has his hand on Aneesa's arm and they are smiling at each other. She lifts a hand to her mouth and shrugs her shoulders. Samir leans against the work surface. Salah turns towards him.

'Will you fetch some water with you, *habibi*?' he asks.

*   *   *

Samir goes through his father's things a few days after
Salah's death. Inside a dresser drawer he finds a piece
of paper with Aneesa's address and telephone number
in Beirut on it. He realizes that he will have to
either call or write and let her know what has
happened but for some reason cannot bring himself to
do it just yet.

'She is here on her own,' Salah had said when he first
told Samir about her. 'She is delighted at meeting someone
from back home.'

'*Baba*, she is only young, after all,' Samir told Salah,
worrying that his father was growing too attached to
Aneesa.

'Yes, she is, thank goodness.'

Time to go home, Samir mouths the words silently to
himself. He has just had dinner in a restaurant not far
from home and is ready to leave. He places his drink on
the table in front of him and reaches for his raincoat.
When he gets to the door and sees the rain tapping at
the window, he goes back to where he was sitting and
picks up the umbrella he left behind.

In the street, he steps into a puddle of murky water.

'Now look what you've done,' Samir mutters angrily
to himself, gripping tightly at the open umbrella as he
walks.

Despite the rain, he decides to go home on foot and
surges forward. With his head held down, all he can see
are legs rushing past on the pavement and the inverted
beams of car lights through water.

He feels a time will come when one thing alone will

turn his head; not the vagaries of wealth, nor beauty in a woman, but something else, something more like an end to regrets, a sudden, destined peace.

When Mother reached out for me, Samir begins to no one in particular, my hand as she held it felt like a shell that had been wrapped in silk, so weightless was her touch. We would stroll along the pavement, stepping carefully off it when we had to cross the street, and I would watch our feet move, her stride slightly wider than mine and my own legs taking little steps forward, skipping when the pace demanded it, and if I tripped, I would feel the pull at my arm, my body being lifted for a moment, floating, before resting on the ground once again.

He stops to take a breath and sees a poster of sea and nubile girls on the sand in a travel agent's window. I have imagined myself, Samir says to the shifting multitude around him, on a Mediterranean land standing in the sun, where moments such as these flow like water and all through the valley trees grow like rivers where the river has once been.

Samir and Aneesa continue to meet, once or twice for coffee and then at a restaurant near Samir's office for lunch. He is aware of his attraction to her and also of a niggling desire to figure her out, the reasons behind his father's fascination with a young woman who is in many ways unexceptional. Every time Samir has telephoned Aneesa and told her he wants to talk about Salah, she has agreed to meet him. Still, Samir is not certain she believes his excuse. Perhaps, he sometimes likes to think to himself, she is as interested in me as I am in her.

Today, he is speaking more easily to Aneesa, feeling less nervous. He asks her fewer questions and and decides to talk about himself instead.

'Sometimes I feel I lack insight,' Samir says between mouthfuls of salad. 'You know, the ability to see beyond the obvious, to read people.'

Aneesa sits across from him with a frown on her face so that he feels she is really listening to him. He lets out a loud sigh and continues.

'Do you ever remember someone just as a feeling, rather than a face? It happens to me all the time, especially with the people I haven't really figured out – you know, the mysterious ones.'

He laughs and waits for her to do the same but she does not.

'Like you, for instance,' Samir says. 'I feel a distant anxiety, something I know I have not quite grasped yet, and then I realize that I'm just thinking of you. Sometimes, I don't realize this for several hours or even days, and all the time I'm experiencing this underlying fear. Strange, isn't it?'

'What are you afraid of?'

But he has no answer to this. He shrugs his shoulders and looks down at his plate. She touches his shoulder with her fingertips and he watches a smile slowly lift the contours of her face.

'I think of you too, Samir,' she says quietly.

He feels slightly flustered.

'My father hasn't told me very much about you,' Samir says. 'It's difficult, isn't it? To know just where to start, to work out what the important things about your life really are.' He puts his knife and fork down and looks directly at her. 'If you could tell me just one thing about yourself, what would it be? I mean, I suppose I'd have to say leaving Lebanon made me a different person, saved me in a way because it opened up my life and my horizons. Made me more flexible because I found myself in an entirely different environment. If you asked me the question, that is.'

Aneesa's face goes still. He had not realized that such a thing could happen, a sudden and certain freezing of movement in the eyes, not a ghostly look, but an immobility with certainty in it, clarity at the edges.

'And I would say . . .' she begins. 'I would say that I once lost a brother.'

He has left his father alone with the nurse for the first time since Salah's illness and is surprised that he does not enjoy the freedom of it more. When he gets home, carrying bags of groceries, his first impulse is to rush to Salah's bedside to make sure he is all right. Instead, Samir goes into the kitchen, sets the bags on the worktop and puts the kettle on before going to his father.

Salah is sitting up in bed holding up the Arabic newspaper Samir bought him the day before, both arms opened wide. The nurse, a young man with a gentle manner, is standing beside him, pointing to different items in the paper. They do not notice Samir.

'Can you read this headline for me?' The young man asks.

Salah speaks out loud, the words running into each other a little, but they are comprehensible nonetheless.

'How about this one? What does it mean?' The nurse points to another headline.

Salah leans forward slightly, reads out loud and delivers a rough translation afterwards.

Samir holds his breath and remains absolutely still. He has not heard his father put complete sentences together since his stroke and is afraid of interrupting the flow of words. Salah's voice rises and falls rhythmically, the patient young man standing quietly beside him so that the two of them seem framed by the light coming in from the window, while Samir stands out of sight, trembling helplessly in the doorway.

Samir sits at his father's desk in the living room doing his homework when his mother comes in and looks over his shoulder.

'You'll have to work very hard to get into university overseas,' she says, patting him on the back.

Salah puts down the newspaper he has been reading.

'Overseas?'

Huda comes round the desk and sits next to her husband on the sofa.

'He's not staying here,' she says firmly.

Samir looks from one to the other of his parents and says nothing.

'What's wrong with our universities?' Salah asks.

'I want something better for our son.'

'So do I, *habibti*, but we have an excellent university over here.'

Huda shakes her head.

'Salah, you know I've always planned for him to leave this country and have a proper future.'

'But this is his home. This is where his future should be.'

Samir feels sorry for his father. His mother, he knows, is bound to get her way in the end. Huda has always talked about him leaving once he grew up but now the idea seems more real than it has ever been before. The thought of being somewhere different where no one knows him excites him.

'We'll talk about this later,' Samir hears his father saying. 'Just get on with your work now, son.'

Aneesa is looking flushed as she steps through the door.

'I practically ran over here from the bus stop, it is so cold,' she tells Samir, her voice slightly breathless. 'This jacket is never quite enough. How are you, Samir? Is Salah upstairs?'

'No, we're in the living room and the fire's going already. Why don't you go inside and I'll bring the tea in?'

It is Saturday afternoon and when Samir found out earlier that Aneesa was coming to visit, he had asked if he could stay. Now he is not so certain that it was the right thing to do.

'Thank you, *habibi*,' Salah says when Samir walks into the living room with the tea tray. 'Ah, you forgot the biscuits, Samir. I'll go and get them, shall I?'

'You don't take sugar, do you?' Samir asks Aneesa as he pours the tea.

She shakes her head. He hands her a cup, pours one for himself and sits back in the armchair by the sofa. The fire is big and warming and emits a pleasant burning scent whenever a wisp of smoke escapes into the room.

'Do you remember yourself as a child?' Aneesa asks him.

165

Samir wonders what is taking his father so long.

'Of course I do.'

'How?'

'What do you mean?'

Aneesa shakes her head and snorts slightly.

'What do you think you were like?'

Fearful, shy and arrogant sometimes, as boys will be for no other reason than to hide their hurt pride. He had also been secretive, not in a sinister way but out of a desire to keep something for himself and from his ever-present parents.

Samir shrugs and smiles at Aneesa just as Salah returns with the plate of biscuits.

'Did your son keep secrets as a boy?' Aneesa asks Salah. She is smiling and Samir feels a sudden irritation.

Salah passes the plate first to Aneesa and then to Samir.

'Stop teasing him, Aneesa,' he says. 'My son has a tendency to be easily hurt.'

Samir looks at his father.

'Me?'

Salah bites into a biscuit.

'I always wanted more children, you know,' he says in a conversational tone so that Samir cannot tell if his father is speaking to him or to Aneesa. 'Huda believed it was because I thought she and Samir were somehow not enough for me but it wasn't like that at all.'

Samir clears his throat loudly and hopes his father will not continue.

'There were many things my poor wife never understood about me,' Salah goes on.

*   *   *

The day of the funeral is sunny and warm for autumn. Samir sits in the limousine that follows the hearse to the cemetery. The interior of the limousine is spacious but sombre and Samir is glad when they arrive and he can finally get out.

It is more like a park than a cemetery, he thinks as he follows the pall-bearers to the grave. The trees are awash with colour: reds, yellows and golds; and dead leaves crunch beneath his feet as he walks. The air is also beautiful, clean and with only the suggestion of coolness in it. In the distance is a pond with ducks floating on it. This day is so perfect that there seems no place for grieving, Samir thinks to himself. He takes a deep breath. I wish you could see this, *baba*. You would love it here.

When he gets home later that evening, Samir walks around for a few moments with the lights still off. He goes into the kitchen and opens the two windows opposite the counter very wide, just like Salah used to. Then he pulls at the refrigerator door and looks inside. He pulls out cheese, Arabic bread and two cucumbers that he washes under the tap. He takes out a knife and plate and sits at the work surface. From here, he can hear the night but it cannot see him. He cuts a piece of the cheese, wraps it in the bread and eats it noiselessly. Then he picks up a cucumber and takes a large bite of it.

If Father were here . . . Samir begins. If I were Father, what would I do now? He puts down his sandwich and stands up, pushing his stool back. Then he walks back to the refrigerator and opens its door slightly so that the inside light shines through into the kitchen. He suddenly thinks of Aneesa, how he would often find her in the kitchen when he came home, chatting to Salah as he cooked, both of them seemingly content. He realizes once again that he should let her know of his father's death. Perhaps I should wait until I go back home and see her, he finally decides

Samir walks back to the stool and sits down. When he picks up his sandwich again, he realizes that the refrigerator light has followed him to his seat. He bites into his sandwich and sighs out loud.

Beirut has never felt so familiar. Samir is as comfortable walking the streets here as he is wandering around his own home. He stops himself sometimes, in front of a shop on a commercial street or on the Corniche over-looking the sea, and wills himself to think of refuge else-where, the streets and byways of much larger cities perhaps, but he cannot. The variety of sounds and smells are recognizable now, he realizes, as are the faces that he sees, dark and well defined like his own. But it is a same-ness that annoys him too, so empty is it of the possibility of standing out from the rest.

He remembers walking down Hamra Street with his mother as a very young child and seeing a tall, blonde woman in a red dress approach from the other side. It seemed to him then that all the buildings and all the people around him had turned to black and white except for that woman whose vibrancy and colour were palpable. She was different from anyone he had ever seen and made his heart beat very fast. He had stopped suddenly, pulled down hard on his mother's hand and let out a loud scream, so that Huda had to bend down and put her arm round his shoulders.

'Shush, *habibi*,' she whispered in his ear. 'Don't cry now. No one is going to hurt you.'

The contrasts that he sees these days are only in his own mind: the noise, people and apparent confusion that now surround him compared to the calm that he has relinquished elsewhere; the extent to which he can distinguish himself here measured against the certain success he so willingly left behind. If he concentrates hard and asks himself what he has gained by returning, nothing comes immediately into his thoughts, only a measure of reticent optimism that there is more to come, that he is waiting to step further into an existence that will prove rewarding and less fearful.

Just before going to bed every evening, Samir stands at the edge of the enclosed balcony of his flat and puts his head out of the window, closing his eyes and leaning slightly forward so that he is closer to the outside world than he would otherwise be. Then he lets the sensations associated with a Beirut night engulf him, wet sea breezes and exhaust fumes, distant lights and the clicking of feet on pavements and a certain confidence in the air that comes from being thrown into life with no forewarning and no chance for redress.

He is lying down on the back seat of the car, listening to his parents talk about him. They have been to Tripoli in the north to visit the citadel there and are now on their way home. Samir had been happy climbing the ancient walls and running down the dirt paths between the ruins with his parents trailing behind. At one point, when they were well out of sight, he had been able to imagine he was all alone in a strange place seeking great adventure.

He feels his mother reach for the small blanket she

always keeps on the back seat and cover him with it.

'He's fast asleep,' Huda says.

The steady movement of the car is lulling him into closing his eyes but he wills himself awake.

'I think he had a good time today, don't you?' Salah chuckles quietly.

Samir waits for his mother to say something but she doesn't.

'We should have had another, you know.'

He holds his breath and feels his body tense up.

'Whatever for?' Huda replies.

When he lets his breath go, he does it slowly so that his parents do not hear him. He wishes he could sit up and look out of the window but snuggles further underneath the blanket instead.

'I mean he would have had a brother or sister. Someone to be with him later on.'

When they get home, Salah lifts him out of the car and carries him upstairs to his bed. Samir does not let his father undress him.

'I want *mama*,' he cries, remembering what his father had said in the car and pushing Salah away.

Huda comes in and puts Samir's pyjamas on, pushing his arms and legs into them a little roughly. Salah remains in the doorway, a look of surprise on his face, and murmurs so Samir can hardly hear him.

'He's just tired, that's all,' Salah says. 'Go to sleep, *habibi*. Go to sleep.'

Aneesa tells him she is leaving. It is a cold day in winter with little light and people scurry around in thick coats and gloves. They are standing at the bar of a sandwich shop and looking out through a huge glass window at the world outside.

He asks her why.

'Because it's time,' she says, shrugging her shoulders and shifting slightly on her feet. 'I've been away for too many years and I've never really belonged here anyway.' She gestures at their surroundings. 'The war has been over for a while, Samir. The future there seems hopeful now and many people have started going back.'

She has on a black woollen jacket and a scarf that makes her neck disappear into its folds. She has taken off her gloves and placed them by her plate.

Samir looks away for a moment and then back at Aneesa again.

'What will you do there?' he asks.

'They need translators even more than they do here. I'll find plenty of work.'

Samir takes a sip of water and clears his throat. He feels brave.

'I wasn't talking about work.'

Aneesa is aware of his discomfort and waits for him to continue.

'I mean what about your life?'

'There's life there, Samir. There always was.' She looks at him, her face suddenly clouded, and presses her lips together. 'Why are you always so negative about home?' she continues.

There are many things that frighten Samir but home is not one of them. He knows he would not be prepared to face Beirut and his past again after all this time. She is brave, he thinks, and then feels uncertain about what to say next.

'Your mother is there on her own?' he asks quickly.

Aneesa nods.

'She'll want you there with her, I suppose.'

'Perhaps not. She thinks I've made a safer life for myself here.'

'She's not pushing you into moving back?'

'You're surprised that I should still choose to return anyway?'

Samir puts his cup down and looks out at a grey street and darkening sky.

'What about Salah?' he finally asks.

'He has you, doesn't he?' Aneesa's tone is sharp.

Samir feels a sudden anger and realizes it is not so much with Aneesa as with himself.

'It's not the same,' he says quietly.

'Then maybe it's time you started taking care of him, Samir. Maybe you're the one he really needs.' Aneesa grabs her gloves and starts to put them on. 'I have to go,' she says.

She turns away and does not see him wave goodbye to her as she walks.

There is a café that he likes to go to, on the other end of the Corniche and close to the new lighthouse. It is perched on rocks that jut out into the sea and is nearly empty in the early mornings. At this time of the year, tables on the terrace are removed and Samir sits underneath a large green canopy with clear plastic around its edges. He looks out at the sea and two fisherman standing on rocks where the waves lap just beneath their feet.

Sometimes he will sit for a couple of hours because there is so much to think about and the quiet here is a great comfort. When he signals to him, the waiter approaches with more hot water and a fresh teabag, but otherwise Samir is left entirely alone.

He has come to think of this place as providing a necessary interlude from the questions that continue to haunt him, but still they come, unexpectedly and with a kind of intensity that he feels unable to handle.

When and how exactly had he lost the people and places that once defined him? Samir wonders. I am so-and-so's son; I live in such-and-such a place. Yet this moment, tea glistening in my cup and outside the persistence of a flailing sea, is all I have. He reaches for his sandwich and unfolds the flat bread so he can look inside. He smiles to himself: they have added the mint this time. He wraps the sandwich up again and takes a generous bite. The mint has a strong, refreshing taste and the *labne* is slightly salty, just as he has always liked it.

When Samir looks towards the sea again, he sees one of the fishermen throw back his line. The man's arms swing far behind him, and as he brings the line forward again, over his head and back into the water, Samir imagines he can see the arch it has made lingering in the air for just a moment, hesitating there, then splintering before finally falling into the waves below.

Salah sits folding the laundry and putting it in neat piles on the kitchen table. He has combed back his hair so that, in profile, it looks to Samir like a white semi-circle that arches over his face; and as he leans forward, his lips pressed tightly together with concentration, the outline made by his back and his shoulders, which are

173

hunched forward, creates another, equally poignant, curve.

Samir walks up to his father and places a hand on his arm. Salah looks up.

'Ah, you're home, son. Did you have a good day at work?'

'Why don't you leave those for the housekeeper to do when she comes in tomorrow?'

'She never does it properly, you know that. Besides, I enjoy folding things.' Salah laughs and gestures to his son with a hand towel. 'Let me get you something to eat.'

'Not yet, *baba*. I'm not really hungry,' he says. 'I saw Aneesa today.'

Salah looks up, his eyebrows slightly raised.

'Oh?'

'Did you know that she's planning to leave?'

'She's going back home.'

Samir looks closely at his father.

'Aren't you going to try to persuade her not to?'

Salah begins to fold shirts, stacking them up on top of each other and patting each one before he starts on another.

'I told her that if what she really wants to do is go back home, then she should definitely do it.'

'But why?'

'We all have to one day, Samir.'

'Have to what?'

Salah pushes his chair back and stands up. He folds one arm close to his chest and begins placing the laundry in the crook of it. Then he picks up a pile of towels in his right hand.

'When you were a boy,' he begins, 'you kept a small torch in the drawer of your bedside table. Your mother said you wanted it there to read after bedtime.' Salah continues as he makes his way out of the kitchen and Samir strains to listen. 'But I used to watch you light up the ceiling with it and hum yourself to sleep just when the night became too dark for comfort.'

The sick room smells of disinfectant and talcum powder. Samir covers his father with an extra blanket and opens one of the windows. Then he decides to tidy up the bedside table, lining the bottles of medications against each other and taking the half-filled glass of water and a dirty teaspoon into the kitchen.

When he returns, his father is still asleep, his bottom lip slightly open and his head to one side.

Samir readjusts the pillow for Salah and sits by the bed to look out of the window. Although it is spring, the air is still cool and some of the trees in the park have not yet filled up with green shoots. He does not think his father will be up for a walk today. He has seemed more frail than usual lately.

Samir leans forward and smooths the blanket over his father's legs in the hope that it will wake him but he remains asleep.

I am lonely without him, Samir realizes as he sits back in his chair.

He watches for passing cars and listens to the even sound of Salah's breath and, as he attempts to align it with his own, feels tears well up in his eyes and fall down his cheeks.

* * *

It is raining so hard that the streets are flooded and cars and people must wade their way through the water. Stepping out into the street, Samir sees the rain slanting sideways with the strong wind; the palm trees on the Corniche are leaning too and the sea is a mass of turbulent waves.

He is wearing a long raincoat and an old hat of his father's that he found in the flat but his shoes are flimsy and he must tread carefully as he crosses the wide, tree-lined road and steps on to the pavement above the water. He loves the smell of rain mixed with the musty scents of the sea and the cliffs that fall towards it. He walks quickly until he remembers that there is nowhere he must go.

Samir has felt the connection between his father and himself as something unstoppable. Yet with Salah's death there is a sudden fading around Samir, as if he was once bathed in light and is now falling into darkness, the lines of his features and body slowly dissolving into a gloom. He cannot see the truth in the old adage that those who die live on through the ones they leave behind. He continues instead with thoughts of his father into the future, wondering how Salah's heart rejoices at being back home and seeing Salah standing on the enclosed balcony of their home watching his son as he walks.

Samir senses the subtle motions of death, the end of touch or sidelong glances, and this unmistakable movement towards indecision brought on by his father's absence. There is nothing and no one, it suddenly comes to him, that really ties me to this place, so that instead of freedom, he is now overcome with despair.

He sits on one of the stone benches that line the wide pavement and stares out at the sea. The Raouche Rock juts out of the water in a huge grey arch covered with green moss. It appears, at first, to be moving, the lines and planes of its surfaces stretching into the air and everywhere around it or dropping down in one swift descent into the water. He wishes he could stand at the top of the rock and gesture towards the horizon like an undisguised prophet and for one moment thinks he sees himself there, the belt of his raincoat undone so that the hem of the garment reaches well below his knees, a small figure, hatless, his hair dripping with rain and behind him hints of an absent sun.

PART SIX

Aneesa is sitting in a pavement café on Hamra Street. The white vinyl tables and orange plastic chairs remind her of a once vibrant Beirut. This is where the country's thinkers and artists used to meet, enjoying a freedom so real it went unnoticed until it was unceremoniously taken away during the war and now in its aftermath. Today there are a journalist or two here and a novelist she recognizes whose pipe and halo-like hair give him the appearance of an eccentric.

Aneesa orders coffee and opens the newspaper she has brought with her out on the table. For a moment, she is distracted by the movement around her, noise and activity that is too familiar to ignore. She looks at the faces of passers-by, their brown hair and dark eyes and skin that is somewhere between pallid and fair. Everyone here, she suddenly thinks, looks just like me.

'You're smiling.'

She looks up.

'Samir!'

He has not changed much, a little older but with the same anxious eyes and earnest expression. Aneesa stands up and lays a hand on his shoulder.

'You finally came,' she says.

Samir had not expected to find her like this and feels nervous and unprepared. He wonders if his hair is tidy and lifts a hand to smooth it back into place.

Aneesa gestures to the chair opposite hers.

'How long have you been back? Is Salah here too?'

Samir sits down, his heart beating fast. He feels a rising panic at having to tell Aneesa the truth and wishes he had had the foresight and the courage to do it earlier.

The waiter brings Aneesa's coffee. She does not reach for it and sits waiting for Samir to speak. When he says nothing and puts his head down so she can no longer see his eyes, Aneesa understands.

'Tell me, please.'

Samir looks up and shakes his head.

'I wanted to let you know,' he begins quietly. 'It all happened so quickly. He was only ill for a short while.'

He feels a sudden stab of pain and puts a hand to his chest. It takes him a moment to realize that he is only relieved at finally feeling able to talk about his father's death. When he looks into Aneesa's eyes and sees the tears forming there, he pauses before continuing.

'I'm sorry. I was so distraught, I . . .'

'I should have known about it right away.' She puts out a hand to lay it on the table and accidentally touches his. The noise around them recedes and she is suddenly aware of herself and of Samir too, the two of them leaning towards each other, and of the sound of their breath. 'When did it happen?' she asks.

'It was some time after you left. He had a stroke last December and only lasted a few weeks after that. I should have called you before he died, I know. Then when you didn't contact us, I just let it go. '

She shakes her head and sniffs again.

She sees how it might have been an ordinary day when she went about her business as usual, nothing that distinguished it from the rest, nothing to signal the sudden change in her life. Was it just around the time when they were calling each other less and less, when she realized she would have to put thoughts of her other life behind her and just get on with things here?

'I need to know more, Samir.'

Aneesa's voice is getting louder. He tells her the date and time of Salah's death and realizes that they are emblazoned in his own memory for ever.

'You were with him?' Aneesa asks.

Samir nods.

'At home.'

She tries to remember where she was at the time, early evening in Beirut, sunlight a recent memory and nothing to look forward to but the dark. She pictures Salah lying down on the living-room sofa, his eyelids closing gradually as he stares into the fire and his heart, beating to a slower rhythm, suddenly ceasing in that brief instant before he can begin to sigh with pain or relief.

'Where is he now?' Aneesa asks.

Samir has a vision of his father sitting at the table across from theirs. He is looking the other way but the gracefulness in the way he holds his head is instantly recognizable. Samir rouses himself and sits up straight in his seat once again.

'What do you mean?'

He watches her close her eyes for a moment and then open them again.

'You had him buried over there?' she asks.

He nods. He thinks he sees impatience cross her face and feels a momentary anger. The man at the table next to theirs turns around and Samir looks at him. He is nothing like Salah.

Something has been lost, Samir thinks to himself, something that cannot be immediately retrieved. He looks down at his hands, folded neatly over each other on the table, and cannot imagine what it might be.

Around them, the café is suddenly filling up and the sound of chairs scraping across the pavement fills their ears. Aneesa sighs and reaches for a tissue from her handbag. She cannot understand why she should now feel comforted by Samir's silence and then realizes it is because she is reminded of Salah, of the way he would sometimes stop talking, as if pausing between thoughts, until they had both forgotten what they wanted to say and it no longer seemed to matter anyhow.

Aneesa is getting used to waking up just before dawn. She puts on her slippers and gets up. In Bassam's room, Ramzi is sound asleep and Waddad does not call out from her bedroom. Aneesa shuffles quietly into the kitchen and turns on the overhead light. She fills up the kettle from a bottle of mineral water on the kitchen work surface.

At the first sound of the call to prayer, Aneesa puts

the kettle on the stove and walks to the window. The mosque is not too far away and the loudspeakers are directed towards the back of the building where the kitchens are located. She feels an initial irritation at the high volume of sound and then the *muazzin*'s voice, intensely nasal but clear, begins to soothe her. It moves through the night and the distance and arrives, unwavering, at her window. Perhaps there are others like me, awake and listless, Aneesa thinks. But they are praying now, kneeling towards the east and whispering secret words that only the heavens will hear.

She pours the hot water into her mug, on to the teabag, and waits a moment or two for it to brew. In her dream, Salah had been lying down in a bed this time, a sheet drawn up to his chin so that only his face showed as if illuminated by the whiteness that surrounded it, his mouth stretched in a formal smile that somehow emanated warmth. She had looked down at him and smiled, longing to touch him but sensing that she must not.

Knowing for certain that Salah is no longer alive reminds Aneesa of the days that followed her father's death. She had wept but known that at any moment she could have stopped and picked up the comforting routine of school and home life. It had, she suddenly realized, seemed just then like nothing more than an interruption and it was only some time later, when she understood that her father would no longer take her hand and gently squeeze it in a silent hello or help her with her homework in the evenings or sit in the armchair in the living room watching the television, that his absence became real.

Aneesa throws the teabag out, picks up her mug and walks out of the kitchen, turning the light off as she goes.

Once in her bedroom, Aneesa shuts the door and puts on the bedside lamp.

Once, as they stood side by side waiting for their bus to arrive, Salah had taken off a glove and slipped his hand into hers. They had not looked at each other, clasping their fingers together tightly, bare palms pushing against one another, Aneesa wanting to cry out and then the bus coming into view so that she could finally let go and run up the stairs to the upper deck with Salah coming up slowly behind her.

She lies back down on her bed and turns out the lamp. Can ours still be called an enduring friendship? she asks the darkness. Now that he is gone?

Waddad goes into Ramzi's room and taps him gently on the shoulder.

'Come on, *habibi*,' she says quietly. 'Time to wake up. Your breakfast is ready.'

Ramzi grunts and rolls on to his back. He opens his eyes and grins when he sees Waddad so that she realizes he is still young enough to enjoy waking up in the morning. She ruffles his hair.

'Come to the kitchen when you're ready and we'll eat.'

Ramzi comes to stay only at weekends, spending the remaining part of the week at the orphanage where he attends school. Waddad misses him when he is not there but sees him when she goes up to the orphanage to do her volunteer work during the week.

'Is Aneesa still asleep?' Ramzi asks when he walks into the kitchen.

'Sit down, *habibi*.' Waddad motions to a chair at the

breakfast table. 'Yes, she was up during the night and didn't get much sleep.'

She sits down to eat with Ramzi who scoops a dollop of *labne* on to his bread and places a black olive on top of it. Waddad dips a piece of bread into a mixture of thyme, sesame seeds and olive oil and pops it into her mouth.

'What are we doing today?' Ramzi asks. 'Is Aneesa taking me somewhere?'

'What would you like to do?'

Ramzi shrugs his shoulders.

'Shall I go and wake her up now?' he asks.

'No, no. Let her rest a bit. Why don't you take your bicycle downstairs and play until Aneesa wakes up? Have you had enough to eat?'

Ramzi pushes his chair back, and goes to fetch his bicycle. He wheels it out of the front door and into the lift. Once on the ground floor, Ramzi goes to a nearby car park that overlooks the main road. Although the sea is just on the other side of the road, he is not particularly interested in it. He is ten years old and there are too many other things, like his new bicycle, that intrigue him. He jumps on to the bike and begins to ride around in circles and loops, then he tries lifting the front wheel up as he balances on the other. He manages to stay up for about a second or so. If only one of my friends from school were here to see me, he thinks. Maybe I should ask Waddad if I can bring a friend with me next weekend or if I can take the bike up to the orphanage for the week. So far, she has not said no to anything. Aneesa is a little more difficult to handle.

From the balcony, Waddad keeps an eye on Ramzi. He

pedals fast towards one end of the car park and suddenly swerves so that he and the bicycle fall on the ground. Waddad winces and watches until Ramzi picks himself up again and gets back up on to the seat of the bicycle.

'He loves that bike, doesn't he?' Aneesa comes up behind her mother and looks down at the car park.

'Good morning, *habibti*. Did you finally manage to get some rest?'

Aneesa nods.

'Are you planning on doing something with Ramzi today?' asks Waddad. 'I think he'd like to spend time with you.'

Aneesa pulls her dressing gown more tightly around her and sips at the cup of coffee she has brought with her. It is exactly as she likes it, strong and bitter. As a child, her father would sometimes let her have a taste from his own cup and was always surprised when she asked for more. Children aren't supposed to like coffee, he'd say with a smile.

'Salah has died,' she blurts out.

'Salah?' Waddad begins. She looks anxiously at her daughter and leans over to lay a hand on her arm.

'I've told you about him, *mama*.'

Waddad shakes her head.

'Your friend? In London?'

'I saw his son Samir. He's back here now, staying in their old flat.' Aneesa gestures to the further end of the Corniche then drops her hand. 'It happened a few weeks ago,' she continues.

'I'm sorry. I didn't realize you were still thinking of him.'

In the back of Aneesa's mind is an inkling of what lies

188

ahead, a reluctant sadness perhaps, or an awakening that will feel like the sky opening above her, pushing outwards until she can lift herself upwards too. Now, standing on this dusty balcony, the damp air around her, Waddad to one side and in the street below a young boy who would be her brother, Aneesa understands that it will always be like this, that the connections she makes on this onward journey of her life will never leave her, touching her skin's surface like a gentle mist that comes and then recedes.

'Neither did I, *mama*,' Aneesa says quietly.

'And this boy lives with you now?' Samir asks.

Aneesa shakes her head.

'He only comes to stay at weekends.'

They are taking a stroll on the Corniche. Since early morning the sun has shone intermittently and only moments ago, they saw lightning flash on the water and heard the claps of thunder that followed. Very few people have ventured out in this weather and Aneesa and Samir are enjoying their almost solitary walk.

'Reincarnation,' Samir says. 'I didn't think people believed in that sort of thing any more.'

An image of the old sheikh of her childhood flashes through Aneesa's mind. She reaches up and runs a hand over her chin, imitating the way the old man fondled his strangely shaped beard. He's probably dead now.

'It's very important to people who live in the mountains,' Aneesa tells Samir. 'They all think they'll have the chance to return for another lifetime and redeem themselves.'

'And you? Is that what you think too?' Samir turns to look at Aneesa. A lock of hair has fallen over her face and is hiding her eyes and she is pressing her lips together tightly. He wonders if he should change the subject to save her embarrassment at his question but finds himself pressing on with the subject. 'Well?'

Aneesa stops and turns her back to him to face the water.

'Sometimes I would like to,' she begins quietly. 'Imagine it, Samir. Imagine being able to come back again and again, to yourself and those you have loved. Do you know what it would mean?'

Looking out over the grey horizon, Samir thinks he is capable of believing in endlessness and in hope. He waits for Aneesa to continue but she turns abruptly and begins to walk again.

'Still, it's very convenient, isn't it?' she says sharply. 'I mean this denying death. It doesn't bring them back.'

With the next clap of thunder, big drops of rain begin to fall. Aneesa pulls up the hood on her jacket and begins to run ahead with Samir in tow.

Samir has remembered something Salah once told him about Aneesa. It was before his father had fallen ill, when he had just found out that Aneesa wanted to return to Beirut.

'Is it her mother?' Samir asked.

It was Sunday and they were out for a drive in the country, on roads that meandered through green fields and occasional forests.

'She hasn't told me why,' replied Salah.

'But you do know why, *baba*. You must.'

Salah looked out of the window and pointed to a farm-house at the end of a field.

'Seems very isolated out here, doesn't it?'

'*Baba*, I'm just concerned about you. I know you'll miss Aneesa.'

'Yes, I will.'

'Then why do you think she's leaving?'

Salah sighed and looked down at his hands, palms down on his knees.

'It's to do with her brother,' he finally said. 'She wants to get things sorted out. I don't really know.'

'But I thought she came here to start again,' Samir protested. 'I thought she just wanted to get on with her life after the kidnapping.'

'She didn't come here for a new life, Samir.' Salah's voice sounded impatient. 'She came here to run away from it,' he continued. 'She's only just realized that things like that do not leave you.'

Samir recalls the conversation and thinks of the experiences in his own life that will always stay with him, such as Salah's death and this lingering doubt that he might not have understood his father as he should have. He wonders too if in staying away from Lebanon for all those years, even after the war had ended, he had been running away too. It surprises him sometimes to realize how, in some ways, he and Aneesa were very similar.

Seeing Aneesa again, Samir has a new idea of her as a woman with purpose, not in the way his mother had been, focused and determined to the exclusion of everything else, but as someone whose resolve cannot be questioned. He knows Aneesa watches him carefully and compares him, perhaps, to his father, but feels she has nonetheless noted something in him that he has wished for himself: the possibility that one day the gods will also lead him.

Aneesa and Ramzi are in the car park near the flat. They are waiting for the group of boys that Aneesa has seen play here on Saturday afternoons. Ramzi has brought his bicycle and he is riding it in ever-growing circles in the centre of the empty car park while Aneesa stands watching. She has been at a loss to find something for Ramzi to do when he comes to visit and is hoping that the boys will let Ramzi join them. But she is not sure how to go about arranging it. I have never had to deal with this sort of thing before, she thinks to herself.

Aneesa calls Ramzi over.

'Look, I'll talk to the boys when they get here,' she tells him. 'I'm sure they'll be fine about it.'

Ramzi is perched on the seat of the bicycle with one leg on one of the pedals and standing on the other. He shrugs and hops to steady himself. Aneesa waits for him to ride off again but he only looks at her. He has changed in the two years since she first saw him, taller and less delicate-looking, and no longer resembles Bassam so much. He seems, she suddenly realizes, much more real somehow; the small childish hand that grasps the bicycle's handles and the scruffy trainers with their laces half undone, these have become a dear and familiar sight.

'Are you all right?' she asks.

Ramzi gets off the bicycle and wheels it towards her.

'Waddad will be waiting for us,' he says. 'Why don't we just go home?'

Aneesa notices a group of children approaching from the other side of the car park. She begins to lift a hand to wave at them but stops herself when she sees the alarmed look on Ramzi's face.

'Listen, *habibi*,' Aneesa says, suddenly understanding. 'I'm feeling a bit tired. Do you mind if I go home and leave you here? You can make your way back on your own, can't you?'

Ramzi beams at her and nods only briefly before jumping back on to his bicycle and riding towards the children. Aneesa stands there for a moment, looking at him, and is surprised at how pleased she is that he does not stop and look back.

It is the first time that Samir has come to Aneesa's home and he is intrigued at the thought of meeting her mother. But Waddad is not as he had pictured her. She is not a bent old woman nor is she particularly motherly in her manner. Instead, she is small and if not feisty, at the very least energetic, and she seems as interested in him as he is in her. They do not sit in the living room on the tired old sofas he noticed when he walked in, but are standing in the kitchen while Waddad fiddles with a pot over the stove and Aneesa tries to get her attention.

'*Mama*, please sit down. I'll take care of it.'

They sit, Waddad and Samir, at the kitchen table, unsmiling and facing each other. There is nothing awkward in the way she looks at him.

'I've been wondering about you ever since Aneesa told me you were here,' Waddad begins. 'You see, she never talked about you before, only your father. God have mercy on his soul.'

She stops and waits for Samir to say something. He is younger and more vulnerable-looking than she had expected.

'Aneesa meant a great deal to my father,' he says. 'He was sorry when she left. We both were.'

Waddad nods and scratches her head. Her hair is grey and cut close to her head like a cap.

'I thought she'd stay there for ever,' she says with a smile. 'But then you can never tell with my daughter.'

Samir watches Aneesa as she lifts the lid of the pot, dips a teaspoon into the mixture inside and tastes it.

'It's too salty, Mother,' Aneesa says.

Waddad turns around to look at her.

'The stew, *mama*. You've put too much salt in it again.'

Waddad turns back to Samir and shakes her head.

'She's teaching me how to cook now,' she says with a chuckle. 'Why don't you stay and have lunch with us?'

There are many things that Samir thinks about when he is alone, things that console him, like the certainty of another day as morning breaks or the sight of the sea, flat and constant, from his balcony, but these are the comforts that loneliness recalls. Being with people once again, two women in a crowded kitchen filled with meals past and present, with words said out loud and late-night musings, he realizes how silent his days are: spaces between his heart and the surrounding air that he is unable to fill.

'I would love to,' he finally says.

194

Aneesa joins them at the table feeling anxious. She knows her mother is curious to find out more from Samir and is afraid Waddad will say something to upset him.

'Will you stay here, do you think?' Waddad asks. 'In Beirut, I mean.'

'He doesn't know yet, *mama*,' Aneesa says quickly. 'He's got a lot to sort out first.'

'I know. I meant after he's through with all that.'

Samir puts a hand on Aneesa's arm and feels some of her anxiety dissipate through his fingers.

'I'm not sure yet what I will do. I have been going through the flat, my parents' things. It makes me happy at times and at others afraid.'

Waddad nods.

'Everything reminds me of them, even strangers I meet in the street bring back memories of my mother and father, in their look or manner,' Samir continues. 'They are with me here as they have never been before.'

Samir has placed his hands before him, clasped loosely together so that Aneesa can see the tablecloth through the spaces between the curves of his fingers and the hollow between his wrists. Her mother leans forward and looks up at him before she speaks.

'But, *habibi*, that's exactly how you should be feeling.'

The shop is not far from the main shopping street. Aneesa glances at the window display – mannequins in men's clothing, shirts and trousers and leather jackets of an indefinable style – before walking inside. It has been such a long time since they last met that she is not certain she will recognize Khaled, an old friend of her brother's.

The man behind the counter is talking on a mobile phone. He looks up and smiles before ending his conversation and coming towards her. He is of medium height, wears thick glasses and his hairline is clearly receding so that his forehead seems unusually high.

'Hello, Khaled,' Aneesa says.

The man approaches and looks intently at her.

'Aneesa! What a nice surprise to see you here! How are you?' He embraces her and then stretches out his arms to gaze at her. 'Don't tell me you've come back to this godforsaken place when the rest of us are trying to leave,' Khaled says, shaking his head. 'Come and sit down, please.' He pulls out two chairs from behind the counter and places them in the middle of the shop.

'I don't want to get in the way,' Aneesa says as he gestures for her to take a seat. 'I just didn't know where else to find you and then remembered your father's shop.'

'When did you get back?' Khaled asks.

'It's been a while now. I'm staying with my mother. How about you? How is your family?'

'The children are almost grown up now,' he says, shaking his head. 'Twelve and thirteen years old and they're enrolled in the same school Bassam and I went to.'

Khaled had been Bassam's closest friend. They went to school and university together and Aneesa suspected had also been involved with the same political group during the war. She had never quite understood the friendship because the two of them were so different, Bassam an idealist and Khaled with his two feet firmly planted on the ground. But after her brother's disappearance, Aneesa had turned to Khaled for help. When she eventually went away, she had relied on him to deliver the letters to her mother.

'Oh, Aneesa, it must be ages since we last spoke,' Khaled interrupts her thoughts. 'How is your mother? I haven't been to see her in a while. It's my fault, I know.'

'The shop has certainly changed,' she says, looking around her at the well-stocked shelves and rails.

'Would you believe we used to do better during the war? Business is getting more difficult every year.'

The street door opens and a customer walks in. Khaled goes up to him.

'Can I help you?'

The young man says he is looking for a pair of socks in pure cotton and Khaled helps him choose them. As he wraps the socks up and gives the young man his change, Khaled turns to Aneesa.

'I'll just be a moment,' he says.

Khaled believes he knows why Aneesa has come to see him and is glad of having a moment or two with a customer to think about what he will say to her.

'Did you ever find out anything new, Khaled, about Bassam, I mean?' Aneesa asks once the young man has left.

He shakes his head.

'Don't you think I would have let you know if I had?'

'But I wasn't here. I thought . . .'

'No, but Waddad is. I certainly would have gone to her.'

'But you must know something,' Aneesa protests. 'You were his best friend.'

Khaled leans forward and puts an arm over her shoulders.

'I told you everything I knew at the time, Aneesa,' he says gently. 'We looked for him until there was no place else to look, you know that. But it was no use in the end.'

Aneesa gets up, pushing her chair back.

'I keep going over it in my mind, Khaled, and it just doesn't make sense. He can't have disappeared so completely, as though he'd never existed.'

'It doesn't have to make sense, Aneesa. Nothing about the war ever made any sense.

All those deaths, all that suffering, it was madness.'

'You think he was killed?'

Khaled hangs his head and takes a deep breath. He has pictured in his mind so many times what might have happened to his friend. He knows enough of what went on during those terrible years to hope that Bassam had not suffered too much before he died.

'You must think that too, Aneesa,' he says slowly.

'I know he's no longer alive. I know that, Khaled. I just want to know what happened. How it happened. I thought you might be able to help me.'

He stands up and leans closer to her. He had almost forgotten about Bassam's disappearance in the few years since the end of the war and realizes there is something in him that resents being reminded of it now.

'Habibti, we may never know what happened. You have to stop thinking about it, Aneesa, for your mother's sake if not your own.'

Aneesa fetches her handbag from the back of the chair where she left it and puts it over her shoulder.

'In the mountains, they believe that those who die a violent death always return,' she says. 'My mother takes comfort in that.'

'Perhaps you can too,' Khaled says.

Aneesa shakes her head as she steps out.

*   *   *

Aneesa has never thought of her upbringing as different from the rest of her generation but there are things about this new Beirut that no longer seem right so that she sometimes feels out of place where she least expects to.

She loves Hamra Street, as she always did, its smallness that once seemed limitless, its tired poor who reach out for money from their seats on the pavement, the clothing boutiques that do not interest her and the saleswomen who look her up and down; she even likes her awkwardness and the way she knows she no longer fits in among those who have experienced a different Lebanon: all these things make her take comfort.

But lately, walking to her favourite bookshop or sitting in a pavement café, Aneesa senses an unspecified dissatisfaction, a faltering malaise that cannot be shaken off and which she cannot be sure belongs to her alone.

Being with Salah had taught her a great deal, a kind of amazement at the details of everyday life that she seems now to have lost, the ability to view everything delicately as if any roughness even in thought would strip it of its true self.

He offered a different kind of life for her in his stories and in his tenderness, pausing when there was a need to wait for breath and applying the same intent when he spoke as he did when listening. She'd felt at times a light illuminating her confusion so that what would have been arduous became a thing of ease, and what she might have feared she later met with courage. She misses him not because she longs to see or touch him again but because the thought of an empty place where he once stood, of silence where he spoke and blindness where he once saw, of indifference in place of his passion and distance where once there was closeness, devastates her.

She sighs and reaches for the small red radio that once belonged to Bassam, wishing her friend was with her. This, she thinks bending over to look closely at the radio, is what Salah would do. She lifts a hand and slowly turns the tuning dial, her ear listening for an easing of static, here, no not yet, or maybe there, yes, that's clearer, until the voice of an announcer can be heard without interference. There, Aneesa thinks, leaning her head back against the armchair she is sitting in, her eyes closing slowly. That is how Salah would have done it, deliberately and without apprehension at what he might have once missed.

'My mother just wasn't that kind of person,' Samir says, reaching further into the bottom of the cupboard. 'She didn't really have the patience for showing tenderness.'

He pulls out several pairs of women's shoes and places them on the floor. They are so covered with dust that he cannot even tell what colours they are. Aneesa holds out a large rubbish bag and motions for Samir to put the shoes inside it but he hesitates.

'I want to look at them for a minute,' he says. 'Besides, there's more in there. Let me get them all out.'

He is sitting on the floor. His head and the top half of his torso disappear into the cupboard again.

'That's not what I was asking you about,' says Aneesa, still standing with the bag open in her hand.

'What?'

Samir pulls his head out again and looks up at her. His hair has dust on it and he is blinking because the dirt has also gone into his eyes. He sneezes and Aneesa giggles.

'What did you say?'

'I asked you how you felt about your mother when she was alive.'

Samir throws another pile of shoes on the floor and sits up on his knees. Besides the dust, Aneesa can see and smell mould on some of the shoes. She watches Samir pick up a shoe and wipe it with the back of his sleeve. It is black patent leather and has a clip-on satin bow at the front. Samir pulls on this and grunts when it comes off.

'I remember this pair,' he says without looking up. 'She wore them with a black beaded gown that I used to love.'

He turns the shoe to the side and Aneesa notices the thick, high heel and rounded toe. She gasps softly when Samir lifts the shoe up and drops it into the bag.

'They'll all have to go, I suppose,' he says with a sigh. 'None of them is in good enough condition to give away.'

Aneesa lifts the ends of the bag up and opens her arms wider as Samir proceeds to throw the shoes inside. She knows he is finding the task of getting rid of his parents' things difficult and wishes there were some way of consoling him. But for the past two days, he seems to have withdrawn further into himself. He no longer answers her questions directly and often sounds as though he is speaking to himself in an empty room.

'It's this house,' Samir says as he watches Aneesa tie the ends of the rubbish bag together. 'I feel alone in it even when there is someone else here with me.'

Aneesa looks at him as he stands up. He knows he has been especially distant since he first asked her to help him clear up the flat. Sometimes, friendship feels like a skill that he does not possess, so delicate are the bonds that bring people together, so fine the emotions connected to them. He would like to reach out and touch Aneesa's hair but does not dare to.

'Look, why don't we stop for a while?' Samir asks. 'I'll wash my hands and find us something to drink. Just leave the bag there, Aneesa. I'll deal with it later.'

When Aneesa used to imagine herself in this flat, it was as a visitor in Salah's home. She feels his absence here keenly but has no memories of him moving through these rooms, cannot see the lines his footsteps once made or the shadows that preceded them. Instead, watching Samir as he walks out of his mother's bedroom, dejection in his shoulders and in the sigh he leaves behind, she realizes that he is what she will remember most about this place, his seeming helplessness and the sensibility he has sought to hide.

She goes out to the enclosed balcony and, because it is slightly chilly, puts on the jumper that is tied around her shoulders. It is early afternoon and the traffic on the Corniche is not as heavy as it was earlier in the day. Still, the sound of car engines is a definite if distant drone, strangely comforting because it is so much a part of Beirut.

Samir comes out to sit with her.

'Your father gave me a painting before I left,' Aneesa says.

'I remember it. It was one of his favourites.'

'Where did it hang here, do you know?'

Samir shrugs.

'I don't remember where he had it. But it was one of the few things he insisted we take with us to London.'

'I think you should have it now.'

'He meant for you to keep it, Aneesa.'

'I only took it because I promised myself I'd give it back to him once he returned.' She tried to recall details of the painting that now hung on the wall opposite her bed but saw only a splash of bold colour and floating wings that seemed to lift the picture upwards.

'It's an angel, isn't it?' Samir asks.

'Yes.'

Samir shifts in his chair.

'He talked about the painting once after he fell ill,' he says. 'He said it had given him great comfort when Mother died. 'He believed . . .' Samir hesitates.

'Yes?'

But Samir only shrugs his shoulders. Salah had never spoken of religion to Aneesa. Yet he had had a quietness about him that made her think of the enduring silence of an empty church in winter and the exquisite symmetry in the outlines of a mosque against a barren landscape.

'Why do you think he gave the painting to me?' she eventually asks.

Samir crosses his arms in front of him and looks out towards the sea.

'I expect he must have thought you needed that angel more than he did.'

Ramzi likes coming down to Beirut. He enjoys staying in a flat that overlooks the sea and prefers the corners and empty spaces in its rooms to the long, crowded dormitories at the orphanage. As soon as he and Waddad arrive on Friday afternoon, he rushes to the bedroom, puts his backpack down on the floor and goes out again on to the balcony to look down at the empty car park. Then he rushes the hallway and wheels his bicycle to the front door.

'I'm going downstairs for a bit,' he calls out to Waddad.

'It's too late now, *habibi*,' Waddad says as she emerges from the kitchen. 'I don't want you out playing at this time of night.'

Ramzi cannot understand why she should think he would not be safe in the dark.

'But look outside.' He points towards the windows in the living room. 'It's still daytime.'

'Ten minutes then,' Waddad says, shaking her head.

She walks back into the kitchen and puts her apron on. Ever since Ramzi's visits began she has had to think about cooking again, substantial meals that they sit at the dining room table to eat, she and her daughter and the young boy.

Tonight, they will have *kafta*, minced meat mixed with parsley and spices which she spreads out flat in a rectangular pan. She peels and slices a few potatoes and places the pieces on top of the meat, pours tomato paste diluted in hot water over it and puts the pan into the oven, then she goes to the sink and picks up the sponge to clean the dishes and utensils she has just used.

It almost feels like it did when her husband was still around and the children had been young. In her mind's eye, she sees her husband sitting in an armchair in the living room, perhaps watching television or reading one of the leather-bound books he kept on the bookshelf in the hallway. Although he had not been a smoker, he would sometimes puff on a cigar that someone had given him and the waft of smoke would weave its way to the kitchen, around her head and into her hair.

The front door slams shut. Waddad listens for footsteps.

'*Marhaba*,' Aneesa comes up to her and kisses her on the cheek.

'You didn't bring your friend with you?'

'Samir?'

Waddad turns around and nods.

'Didn't think of it,' Aneesa says. 'Here, let me finish the washing up.'

'It's all right, *habibti*, I'll do it. Could you call Ramzi up from downstairs?'

Aneesa puts her handbag on the kitchen table.

'Whatever it is smells very nice,' she says as she walks out.

Looking down at the car park from the balcony, Aneesa watches Ramzi making loops and circles with his bicycle in the fading light. His head is sunk deep into his raised shoulders and though she cannot see his features, she imagines his eyes have squinted into slits with concentration and his top front teeth, still slightly large for his child-mouth, are pressing hard into his bottom lip.

Aneesa leans into the railing.

'Ramzi,' she calls out a couple of times, but he does not seem to hear her.

She takes a deep breath, sticks out her chin and tries again.

'Bassam!'

Ramzi stops, looks up at her and waves but Aneesa is too stunned to respond.

'It's time for dinner,' she finally whispers to no one but herself.

Samir is tidying up the kitchen before going to bed when he hears a knock at the door. Aneesa has been crying, her eyes are red and her hair is dishevelled. Samir motions for her to come in and when she does, she stands for a moment by the front door, her shoulders pushed up towards her ears and her hands clenched in tight fists. He shuts the door behind her and takes her by the arm.

'Come,' Samir says gently. 'Come now, Aneesa.'

They sit side by side on the sofa in the living room with only the side lamp on. It is not cold but Aneesa still has her jacket on. She sniffs loudly.

'I just put Ramzi to bed,' she says.

'That's good.'

'*Mama*'s gone to sleep as well.'

Samir only nods.

'I had to get out of there, you know?'

Samir reaches up and touches Aneesa's hair. It is not frizzy like it was when he first knew her but has waves in it now that end in wisps around her head. He smooths it back and as he does so feels her snuggle into the crook of his arm. This close, he can smell the dampness on her cheeks and hear her breath going in and out. He leans his cheek on the top of her head.

'Samir?' Aneesa looks up and he lifts his head again.

'Yes, *habibti*?'

She sits up and he removes his arm from around her shoulders. They look closely at one another.

'What if you stayed here?' Aneesa begins. 'What if you didn't go back?'

Her eyes, even at this time of night, do not look any darker but rather deeper, as if they had receded further into her thoughts.

'Remember that night we all went out for dinner together, with my father?' Samir asks.

She nods.

'You had on a long black dress and these long earrings.' He gestures towards his own ears and they both laugh. 'I'm sorry, Aneesa, that I didn't tell you then how beautiful you are.'

He leans forward and kisses her tenderly and when he holds her, he can feel her sigh into his body.

Everything has been cleared out of his parents' flat and, despite the still solid walls and the furniture, to Samir it is like an empty shell, although it has occurred to him that the hollowness he now feels might be inside his own heart.

Will I ever be able to live here? he asks himself. Not alone and not with all these memories. He is equally reluctant to let the place go; with it he sees the last tenuous connection with his past vanishing away. Yet there have been times since his return to a much changed city when he has felt himself at one with this new incarnation of Beirut, with the rough, less sharpened parts of it which sometimes make him feel slightly embarrassed as if in merely not understanding these incongruities he can disassociate himself from them.

Beyond his flat, he abhors the obsession with wealth that seems to have taken over everyone here. What happened to the middle classes? he asks himself. Is it the war that drove them away to seek futures that this country can no longer offer them? In returning, he believes he brings with him an accurate judgement of what has become of Lebanon, though Aneesa often faults him on that. What, she says, would you expect from this place after what its people did to it and to each other? He knows there is truth to her question, but is certain as well that something valuable, something Lebanon once possessed in abundance, is absent now and he does not think it will ever return. Perhaps, Samir ponders, I am forcing my own sense of loss on to what I am experiencing today. He is doubtful also that in leaving Beirut for good he would be able to brush this unfamiliar distaste away and thinks that it will haunt him always, even as he tries to disown it.

One morning, standing in the doorway of his parents' bedroom, he is startled by a rush of wind that pushes through the open window pane and rustles the half-open blind. Leaning out to shut the window, his head halfway through it, he sees on the wall beneath, the morning sun moving with the shadows just as it did when he was a child, delighting him yet again. Samir straightens himself up again and stares down at the Corniche. It will go on with or without me, all of this, he thinks to himself.

Unlike Salah, Samir is not accommodating, nor does he encourage in Aneesa an aspiration for greater eloquence. Instead, he often leaves her clinging more tightly to her intransigence as if in doing so she might succeed better in persuading him when, in fact, the exact opposite is true. But she is happy to be with him and this, she thinks, has something to do with their shared past, their mutual knowledge of a loving but puzzling Salah. Together they make firmer Salah's presence in the world until she is no longer so conscious of his disappearance.

This evening, Samir has arranged to take all of them, Aneesa, Waddad and Ramzi, to attend a musical concert in a local theatre. There will be an *oud* player and an accompanying orchestra and Aneesa is looking forward to listening to Arabic music again.

'I didn't even know they held these types of things in Beirut any more,' Samir says once they are all standing in the foyer of the theatre.

He is happy to be in this crowd of people who are clearly accustomed to these sorts of occasions. It is not a large crowd but it is an animated one. Samir has not forgotten how exciting Beirut can be but in his solitude has thought he would never again fit into its exuberance. He reaches out and pats Waddad on the arm.

'How about a cold drink?' he asks her before turning to Ramzi. 'Come on, *habibi*, let's go and get some refreshments for the ladies.'

If Waddad were honest with herself, she would admit that rather than joy, she is suddenly aware of a huge sense of loss. She watches Samir and Ramzi as they walk towards the kiosk, the back of Samir's head slightly flat, looking vulnerable and unappealing at the same time, Ramzi's arms hanging limply by his side because he is unsure how to move in his new jacket. She watches them and wonders why her life is suddenly filled with so many unknowns, people who are practically strangers and situations in which she does not quite fit in. Even Aneesa, in her long red skirt and her hair falling silkily over one side of her face, even her daughter seems distant and unfamiliar tonight.

She also wonders about Aneesa's other life and realizes that her own preoccupation with finding Bassam did not allow any other thoughts to enter her mind, not even those that had to do with her daughter and of what had really happened to her during her time away. Perhaps Aneesa had fallen in love. But if she had had someone, then why did she leave him and return to Beirut? And hadn't Salah been quite old when he died?

Waddad looks down at her feet and feels a slight buzz in her ears. She does not know if she will ever feel whole again. When she looks up, Ramzi is walking towards her with a drink in each hand. She reaches out and touches his hair.

'Thank you, *hayati*,' she whispers so he cannot hear her.

Ramzi sips at his juice and feels the collar of his shirt dig further into his neck. He reaches for his tie and runs a hand down it as he's seen other men do. He would have preferred wearing something more comfortable but Waddad had been so excited about these new clothes that he knew he could not disappoint her.

When a bell rings to call the audience inside, the four of them make their way down to their seats. Samir sits on the aisle seat next to Aneesa with Ramzi in the middle and Waddad at the other end. They take off their jackets and look around. The auditorium is shaped like an amphitheatre and the performers are in the centre with the audience rising in a semi-circle around them. The lights are dimmed and people's voices begin to taper off.

'It feels very intimate, doesn't it?' Aneesa whispers to Samir.

He nods without turning to her so that she has a clear view of his profile outlined against the faint light. It is not a striking face but there is beauty in it, an indication of inner fortitude. She places a hand on his arm and he smiles.

Samir senses that if he looked at Aneesa now, if he were actually to see the happiness that he can feel vibrate so fiercely through her body, there might be an end to indecision. I would simply remain here and begin again with her and the others, tentatively at first and later with stronger resolve. What does place matter, after all, as long as Aneesa is here?

Samir places his hand over Aneesa's and before he can turn to her sees the performers come on stage. There is loud applause as the *oud* player sits on a stool at the centre and places his instrument on one knee. He smiles at the audience and waits for his fellow performers to take their seats before beginning and Samir feels his determination dissipate.

When it begins, the music is so familiar that Aneesa almost jumps up in her seat. The beat, kept by the *derbakke* player to the left of the main performer, is fast and light, and the sound of the *oud* is filled with a tenderness she recalls only from childhood, notes trilling after each other until the whole sounds like water rushing down a rock cliff or clouds shifting across the sky. There is an air of melancholy in the melody that fills the part of her she has always associated with home. She imagines herself, for one moment, on the stage, moving in and around the musicians, diaphanous and light.

She looks at Ramzi. He is nodding as he listens to something Waddad is whispering into his ear. On the other side of her, she senses Samir's pleasure without looking at him, the outlines of his figure already in her memory. Aneesa is suddenly conscious of a connection to these three disparate people as though, for this moment at least, she is the one bond that brings them together. She feels the sharp edges of the music that envelops them move along the surface of her skin, and shudders slightly.

When the music comes to a stop and there is a roar of applause, Aneesa remains still in her seat. Is this, she asks herself, my family now?

Samir and Aneesa have dropped Waddad off at the orphanage and are on their way back down to the coast. Aneesa is driving and has opened the two front windows to let in the clean mountain air.

'Is Ramzi happy here, do you think?' Samir asks.

She is wearing sunglasses and he cannot see the reaction in her eyes.

'I suppose he's used to it by now.'

'I wonder how he feels about Waddad's idea of him?'

Aneesa turns to look at Samir.

'Idea?' she asks abruptly, her eyebrows rising above the rim of her glasses.

'I mean her thinking that he is Bassam. It must be strange for him,' he continues. 'He is just a child, after all.'

Aneesa overtakes the car ahead of them.

'There are some things you don't understand, Samir.'

'You're probably right. I'm sorry.'

Aneesa eases her foot off the accelerator slightly as they begin to descend the hill. She takes a deep breath and looks at Samir again.

'It's all right,' she says softly.

She moves the car further to the right and stops on a ledge overlooking the city. From here, Beirut is merely a cluster of grey concrete buildings. It is not beautiful, Aneesa thinks to herself, despite the sea and the blue sky. She misses the expanses of green, the leafy trees and grass that once fascinated her because they were so different from pine and gorse bush and red dust beneath shuffling feet. She misses the peace she had found overseas, the seeming certainty that she would remain safe as long as she stayed away from Lebanon. Perhaps, she muses silently, I can move to the mountains, to some quiet village where the war has not been, where no one knows me and where I can be alone. She imagines herself in a small house, bending over a wood-fired stove; she is old and alone but happy. Then she laughs at the absurdity of the thought.

'Aneesa?' Samir interrupts her thoughts. He reaches over and touches her hand. 'What are you thinking about?'

'Sometimes you remind me so much of your father. You show the same kind of refined gentleness when you're with me. Loving gentleness.'

He stops caressing her hand and waits.

'But Salah was never in love with me.'

Samir remembers the two of them walking through the front door hand in hand, she with her gloves on, his hands bare and red with cold. They are always smiling when they are together. He is certain she is wrong. He shakes his head.

'It was Salah who insisted that I come back here,' she says and hangs her head.

'He loved you, Aneesa. I am certain of that.'

213

She says nothing.

Samir feels suddenly brave.

'Will you come away with me?' he asks. 'We'll leave here. We can take Waddad back with us, Aneesa. We'll never have to return. We'll be happy.'

She lifts her head and looks beyond him, through the window and at the city she knows is the only home she will ever have. In those hidden streets, around corners and at the end of alleyways, is her family of past and present, her father, her mother and her brother Bassam, the people she will come to know in time, those who will stay, those who will leave and others whose presence and import-ance will fade. From this distance, she can feel the pulse of Beirut and her part in it. She moves the car back on the road and continues the descent down the mountain.

'Let's just go home for now, Samir? Let's just go home.'

Ramzi can feel himself changing, not so that he looks or sounds different but in the way he feels about things and in his manner. He no longer waits on Sundays for his mother to arrive at the orphanage to reclaim him nor does he allow himself to think of his father and the sadness that they have both left behind. Instead, he is happy at the certainty that at the end of each week he will go down to Beirut to his bicycle and to his bedroom, to Waddad and Aneesa and to a sense of home.

In the dorm room where he sleeps, Ramzi spends time on the inside window ledge where the bird cage once sat. The bird died some months ago and though he misses the sound of its voice he is happy to be in its place looking down into the verdant gorge as the other children sleep.

During the day and while in the classroom, he wills himself to focus on the task at hand. When lessons are over he runs quickly out into the playground, feeling the air and the energy push so hard out of him that he imagines they might one day propel him into the sky, over the earth and far away. The things that once mattered, showing the younger children at the orphanage how to play basketball or keeping his half of the cupboard in the dorm room tidy, no longer do, although he is uncertain why.

On the day that his mother finally comes to see him, Ramzi is taken completely by surprise. It is mid-afternoon and he is sitting in the inner courtyard with some of his classmates while the younger children nap indoors. One of his teachers approaches and tells him the directress wants to see him. As he gets up and walks through the familiar archway and across the outer terrace to the office annexe, Ramzi is aware of a sudden but certain quiet surrounding him. He thinks perhaps that it is the lull of the hour, sometime between day and night, between activity and rest. He feels a listlessness gurgle inside him that is akin to premonition. Standing on the terrace for a moment at some distance from the ledge, Ramzi looks to the right so that he sees only the hills and not the valley below. In his mind's eye, the sea that embraces Beirut is not far beyond. Perhaps, he thinks clearly to himself before going inside, this is the right place for me after all.

It is very late but Samir is unable to sleep. He looks at the outlines of Aneesa's body lying next to him and turns on to his back. Once his eyes are used to the darkness, Samir can make out the chandelier hanging from the

215

ceiling. It is made of brass and has a flat disc at the centre with four branches descending from it. On the end of each of them is a glass flower into which a bulb is fitted. The whole thing is very feminine and does not give out very good light.

He remembers the day his mother brought it home with her.

'It's beautiful, isn't it?' Huda had looked at him before turning to Salah. 'For our bedroom, I think, *habibi*, don't you? I just couldn't resist it.'

Salah nodded and looked at Samir.

'I suppose I have no choice, eh?' he asked, smiling, but Samir looked away.

'It's lovely,' Huda had protested. 'You'll learn to love it, Salah, you'll see.'

Samir sits up abruptly. You were right, *mama*, he thinks to himself. Even I have grown to like it.

He looks down to make sure he has not woken Aneesa, then he pushes his pillow up against the wall and leans back against it. He takes a deep breath and looks down at Aneesa again. He reaches out to touch her and when he feels her stir, pulls his hand back again. Outside, there are no sounds coming from the Corniche, and Samir realizes that he is feeling suddenly, inexplicably happy.

Samir is driving them up to the house in the mountains. He has not been there yet and Waddad is anxious to show it to him.

'It belongs to my husband's family now,' she says. 'I suppose we could start going up there again if we really wanted to. I think you'll like it, Samir.'

216

He remembers this road from the trips he took with his parents as a child.

'We used to come up here often,' he tells Waddad, who is sitting next to him in the front seat. 'My mother loved to look at the old houses and I liked filling huge containers with water from the village springs.'

'I promised Ramzi we'd drive across that new bridge they've just built,' Waddad says, turning round to the back seat and smiling at Aneesa and Ramzi. 'Maybe we can do that on the way back.'

'No problem,' Samir says.

She shifts in her seat and pulls the seatbelt down off her neck. Samir insisted that she wear it and it is hugely uncomfortable.

'I'll never get used to these things,' she grumbles and Samir laughs.

Once they get there, Samir drives into the village square. He stops the car and gets out, Ramzi following him. They walk to the spring at the end of a descending flight of steps.

'I've been here many times before,' Samir says.

They watch a man as he holds a plastic water container under the spout of the spring.

'So have I,' Ramzi says. He is standing with his hands in his pockets and is nodding solemnly. Samir wants to laugh out loud but does not want to embarrass the child. He lays a hand on his shoulder.

'Let's find a place to get some water for the ladies,' Samir says.

'Come on then,' Ramzi says. 'I know where it is. I'll show you.'

At the house, Waddad gives Samir the key and asks

him to open the door. Samir looks back at Aneesa but she is wandering around in the bedraggled garden. She must be thinking about her father's roses, he thinks.

Aneesa squats down and tugs at a weed growing in one of the flower beds. She is not certain it is a weed but it is ugly and she feels a sudden need to pull it out. Ramzi squats down beside her.

'What're you doing, Aneesa?'

She throws the weed over to the other side of the garden.

'Nothing,' Aneesa replies.

Ramzi jumps up.

'Let's go round the back and see what there is there,' he says.

Aneesa follows him down a slight incline and to the left of what is actually the front of the house. The garden is even more overgrown here. In the centre of the garden, there are stone benches placed in a circle around a large, round slab of marble. Ramzi steps up on to one of the benches and begins to jump across from one to the other.

'Come on, Aneesa,' he calls to her.

She joins him and they race after one another, round and round the table until she is breathless, laughing.

'Stop, Ramzi. I can't any more.'

He jumps to the ground and shrugs his shoulders.

'I'm going to go explore over there,' he tells her and runs off.

Aneesa tries to catch her breath. She looks up towards the verandah that runs along one side of the house and sees Samir and Waddad standing side by side at one end of it. Waddad is pointing to the mountains in the distance and talking. Samir nods and places a hand on her shoulder. He bends down until his ear is close to Waddad's mouth and when he straightens up again, Aneesa can see the look of concentration on his face. She feels her heartbeat slow down after all the jumping around with Ramzi. Then, still standing on the bench, she turns around and looks in the direction that Waddad is pointing. She sees something glisten all the way across the valley and wonders what it is. She squints slightly and realizes she is looking at the new bridge that her mother had been talking about earlier when they were driving up here. It is so enormous that even from this distance she can see the cars driving across. She looks around for Ramzi but he has disappeared and Waddad and Samir are no longer on the verandah. She steps slowly off the bench and walks back towards the house, suddenly aware of the persistent sound of the crickets hidden high up in the pine trees.

The front door is still open. Aneesa steps inside and shivers at the dampness in the air. We should open up all the windows, she mutters to herself. But the others are nowhere to be seen. In the kitchen, Aneesa stops to try out the tap at the sink. The water comes out in a sudden spurt, murky and smelling of mud.

When she and Bassam decided to camp out in the back garden once, long ago, they had sneaked into the kitchen late at night and raided their mother's larder. It had been Bassam's idea, an adventure that he had included her in despite her young age and the fact that she was a girl. The kitchen had seemed different in the dark with only the faint light from Bassam's torch to light the way. Bassam headed straight for the larder and gestured to her to wait for him, but instead she opened the refrigerator door and looked for something she could take with her. She finally decided on a large chunk of yellow cheese that she knew was Bassam's favourite. Then she felt her brother's grip on her arm pulling her roughly away from the refrigerator. Are you crazy? he had asked. They'll see the light and catch us. There's still so much you don't know!

Aneesa walks out of the kitchen and back through the front door. Then she goes looking for Waddad and the others. It is time to lock up and return to Beirut.

Aneesa leans forward and nuzzles her cheek against Samir's. It is late and they are sitting up in bed talking. She pulls away and looks at him.

'We could fix the mountain house up and spend the summers there,' she says with a smile. 'You probably don't remember how hot Beirut gets in the summer.'

'I remember,' he says. 'I also remember that the beaches here are great at that time of year.'

'I prefer the mountains.'

'Mmmm. Yes, you would. You're a village girl at heart, aren't you?'

They laugh out loud and Samir is delighted to see that Aneesa is blushing.

'Besides,' he continues, 'when we go away, we won't be able to come back here every summer.'

He slips down in the bed and pulls her down with him.

'Samir,' she says as he begins to kiss her. 'Please don't talk about leaving now.' She holds his head in her hands. His face looks smaller and almost childlike this close up.

'You are so different from the nervous man I met all that time ago.'

'How?'

She frowns.

'How am I different?'

She puts her hands down and snuggles further under the sheets.

'You're bolder and more subtle at the same time,' she says. 'It's difficult to explain.'

He wraps his arms around her so that her head fits over his shoulder and he can feel her chin moving against him as she speaks.

'I'm just happy that we're together here for now.' Her voice is a whisper.

When Aneesa tells Samir that she cannot go back with him, he is surprised at how easily he takes the refusal and wonders if he didn't half expect it. He asks her why she will not come and she replies with a question of her own. Why don't you stay here instead, Samir? We can make a home here together.

But he knows that he is not yet ready to live with the hardships of readjustment that would inevitably follow his remaining in Beirut, nor to face the challenges of this love she has brought into his tired life. I don't think I am brave enough for all this yet, Aneesa, he tells her. But you will be soon, I know, is her reply.

Still, she has not said no to being with me, he thinks as he walks on the Corniche late one night. Now that she is settled here, leaving is no longer a choice. It's clearly up to me now.

He looks up at the moon, a thin crescent, its light soft and almost translucent so that the sea ripples only faintly with its reflection, and sighs deeply. If he is honest with himself, he will admit that he has not really thought about the prospect of sharing a home with Aneesa and Waddad in London. What would it have been like? he wonders. Would we have eventually moulded ourselves into a unit of sorts? He shakes his head and walks on. His mother would have disapproved. Being on such intimate terms with relative strangers would have appalled her, he knows. But it seems to him now that Huda would have felt just as appalled at everything he has done since his father's illness and passing. What amazes him is that he no longer cares.

Moving forward, Samir feels immeasurably lighter, as though he has wings to buoy him as he walks. It occurs to him that of all the women he has been involved with, Aneesa is the only one who continues to puzzle him. Is that the case, Samir asks himself, or is it simply that I want so much to understand her? He stops in front of the Raouche Rock and stands at the railing. The Corniche is empty but the street lights are on and a faint din of popular Arabic music is coming from a restaurant a few metres away. He takes a deep breath of the salty air. When he turns his head to the right, he sees the block of flats that Aneesa and Waddad live in. With only a few lights shining through the windows, the building seems abandoned. But Samir cannot think of himself as a thwarted lover nor of Aneesa as cold and unfeeling. I want only to be with her, he says out loud before slowly turning to make his way back to the emptied flat.

*   *   *

Waddad gets back home much later than usual. Aneesa lets her in and leads her straight to the kitchen for dinner.

'I'm not hungry, *habibti*,' says Waddad.

'Mother, you know you must eat. Just try a little for my sake.'

Waddad shakes her head and sits down heavily on one of the kitchen chairs. Then she places her head in her hands on the table.

'*Mama*, what's the matter? Are you all right?' Aneesa puts a hand on her mother's arm and shakes it gently.

Waddad looks up. She is crying.

'Please tell me what has happened, *mama*. Please don't frighten me like this.'

'That woman wants to take him back with her.' Waddad's voice trembles as she speaks.

'Who are you talking about, Mother? What do you mean?'

Waddad moves in her seat so that the chair scrapes loudly against the floor. Aneesa winces at the sound.

'Ramzi's mother has come to take him away from the orphanage,' Waddad says. 'What are we going to do, Aneesa? What are we going to do? God help us!'

Aneesa bends down and embraces her mother. Waddad's shoulders have caved in so that she seems slighter than usual to the touch. Aneesa does know what to say in the way of comforting words.

'Is Ramzi all right?' she finally blurts out.

Waddad pushes her daughter gently away and looks up at her. Aneesa's face has grown smoother and more open with time so that one can almost believe there is nothing hidden behind it. At this moment, it seems to Waddad as if a light is burning through Aneesa's skin.

'You love him too now, don't you, Aneesa?' she says to the younger woman. 'You love Ramzi too.'

Samir does not want Aneesa to accompany him to the airport but he asks if he may come and spend his last evening with her and Waddad.

It is slightly cooler on the balcony where they decide to sit but the air is surprisingly dry and pleasant. Aneesa places a few dishes on the table, *tabboule, hommos, mtabbal* and *mjaddara*, as well as a basket filled with bread. She also brings out a large bottle of water and glasses. She is hoping that her mother will have the appetite to eat.

The traffic on the Corniche is noisy. Samir lifts himself off his chair and looks over the balcony railing. There are cars trying to make U-turns into oncoming traffic, others stop and start inches away from vehicles alongside them and still others beep their horns instead of using their signal lights. He shakes his head and smiles.

'That' – Samir points down to the street – 'will never change.'

Aneesa scoops a spoonful of *tabboule* on to his plate and hands him some lettuce leaves to eat it with.

'Thank you, *habibti*,' says Samir. 'Mmmm. This is delicious and tangy just as I like it.'

Aneesa nods and smiles.

'*Mama*, you have some too,' she says, serving Waddad. 'I'll go and get the cabbage leaves for your *tabboule*.'

Waddad watches Aneesa walk back indoors, then turns to Samir.

'Why are you leaving?' she asks him.

He swallows hard and takes a sip of water before replying.

'I will miss you both very much,' he says.

Waddad dips a piece of bread into the bowl of *hommos* but does not eat it.

'There's very little I can make my daughter do, Samir, but I know she would have stayed with you if you'd let her,' she sighs. 'That would have made me very happy.'

'But I asked her to come back with me, for you both to come with me.'

Waddad looks closely at him and purses her lips.

'That's not the same thing, is it?'

Samir wonders if Waddad can see into him, not just read his mind but look right through the skin and flesh to the bones and organs, if she can measure his pulse with her eyes and with only a thought stop him in mid-breath. He shakes his head.

'I'm hoping to come back one day soon, Waddad. That's all I know right now.'

Aneesa comes out again with half a cabbage in one hand and a plate of olives in the other.

'Did Aneesa tell you about Ramzi?' Waddad asks Samir. He nods.

'Is there nothing that can be done?' he asks.

'I spoke to a lawyer,' Aneesa says. 'If his parents want the boy back, there's nothing anyone can do about it.'

'But he can come to visit?'

'They have promised they'll allow him to come here from time to time. We'll also be able to go and visit him.'

'But if we'd had the money,' Waddad says, scooping *tabboule* into a cabbage leaf, 'we could have paid them off and kept him with us.'

'We don't know that for sure, *mama*. Anyway, even if we could have done it, we wouldn't have wanted to pay for Ramzi to stay.'

Waddad wants to say that she would have done anything to keep him, but she does not.

'Will you still go up to the orphanage for your volunteer work?' Samir asks Waddad.

'I don't know. I'm not too sure of anything right now.'

'Of course you will, *mama*. They need you up there.'

There is anxiety in Aneesa's voice. Waddad simply nods and goes back to eating. Ramzi would have enjoyed this meal and he would have insisted on going downstairs to ride his bike afterwards. The bicycle no longer stands propped up against the wall in the hallway. Waddad had insisted that he take it with him, along with all the other toys and clothes she had given him. He had stood at the door, his hands grabbing the handlebars and simply said thank you for everything. Then he had nodded and gone downstairs to the car where Aneesa was waiting to take him back to the orphanage. Waddad, not wanting to upset him with her crying, had remained upstairs and watched from the balcony as Ramzi and Aneesa carefully placed the bicycle in the boot. To her surprise, just before getting into the car, Ramzi looked up at her and waved. She waved back and sniffed loudly. Moments later he was gone.

'I think I'll go to bed now, *habibti*,' Waddad says. 'I'm feeling a bit tired.'

Samir stands up and they hug one another.

'Thank you for everything,' he says as they both step back.

Waddad nods and goes inside.

It is a good place to be, sitting so high up with the sea

before them and the world too far away to disturb them. Aneesa thinks that of all the things she and Samir have done together here, this evening will be the one she will remember most, perhaps because it is so final, because there is only one way it can end. She reaches for Samir's hand and they sit together, touching, until it is time for him to leave.

Ramzi is sitting in the back seat between his mother and another passenger. It is sunny but cold outside and the car heater, which the driver turned on some time ago, is blowing hot air on to Ramzi's face. He looks out of the window. They have already crossed the border and are now on their way to his mother's village with Ramzi's suitcase and bicycle strapped to the roof of the taxi. Ramzi had asked the driver to put the bicycle in the boot before they set off but the man said it would not fit. Instead, he fetched a piece of rope that looked somewhat flimsy and tied it on top of the taxi.

'Don't worry,' the driver had said. 'It'll be fine up there.'

But Ramzi is still not convinced because he hears the bicycle rattling from time to time as they move and, anyway, what if it begins to rain and it gets all wet and rusty?

They have been on the road for many hours and Ramzi is tired. He turns to his mother.

'How much longer will it be?' he asks her.

'Not too long now,' she replies. 'Sit still, Ramzi.'

'But I'm thirsty.'

She reaches into the plastic bag at her feet and pulls out the bottle of water she filled at the last stop they made. Ramzi has a drink and tries to hand the bottle back to his mother.

'Offer it to the lady next to you,' she says. Then she takes the bottle from him and leans across to the woman passenger. 'Please, have some.'

Ramzi looks out of the window again at the wide fields of violet-coloured earth and the occasional gorse bush on either side of the road. It's very different here. There is no sea; nor are there any real mountains, only low, rocky hills that stand next to each other looking very much alike.

His mother and the passenger are having a conversation.

'He's my eldest,' he hears his mother saying. She pats him on the head and pushes a lock of hair back off his face.

'How old is he?' the woman asks.

Ramzi looks away again. He begins to wonder what Aneesa is doing. It is Saturday and she had told him she might go over to the car park and tell his friends that he had had to go away for a while. They'll probably just go on playing and forget all about me, he thinks, and feels himself getting frustrated.

'He left me with four children to care for on my own,' his mother tells the woman. 'I had no choice but to send Ramzi away for a while and took the other children to my parents' place until I got myself sorted out. Now we'll all be together again.'

'Tsk, tsk,' the woman says.

Ramzi tries to reach for the plastic bag.

'What do you want?' his mother asks, pushing him back against his seat.

'Can't we stop for a bit now, *mama*, and have a look around?'

'We're just turning into the village where your grandparents live,' his mother says. 'Look!' She points to the houses that appear on either side of the road. The terrain hasn't changed, but the one- and two-storey buildings soften the landscape a bit. Some of the houses are made of concrete and look grey and ugly; others are older and made of stone. Ramzi hopes his grandparents' house looks a little better than these so.

'See, Ramzi. This is the entrance to the village. Jiddo and Sitto's place is further along, off the main road. Maybe you don't remember it any more. You were very young last time you were here.'

The car comes to a sudden stop.

'I'll be turning off here,' the driver turns around to tell Ramzi's mother.

They get out and the driver takes the bicycle and suitcase off the roof of the car.

'Can I ride it there?' Ramzi asks his mother.

'I'll take the suitcase,' she says. 'You go on ahead. It's the dirt road on the right.'

He likes the challenge of manoeuvring the bicycle, steering clear of the stones and ditches in the road and the houses on either side of it. Every once in a while he stops to look back and make sure that his mother is following him. They approach a clearing at the end of which Ramzi sees a concrete house with two trees just outside the front door. A man is sitting on a chair underneath one of the trees. As they get closer, the man gets up and starts to wave and Ramzi realizes it must be his grandfather whom he has not seen since he was very young. Ramzi stops and waves back.

'Jiddo,' Ramzi calls out.

His grandfather says something but Ramzi cannot make it out. Soon, Ramzi's brothers and sister come out to meet them.

'He's got a bike!' his sister calls out. 'Look, he's got a bike.'

Ramzi stops and puts one foot on the ground, leaving the other on the pedal. He watches the younger ones approach, with his grandfather and his grandmother behind them. The children are kicking dust up with their feet and his grandparents are smiling. In the distance, there are more of the same hills he'd seen on the road over here. He'll be able to explore them later. Maybe the others will come with him. Ramzi gets off the bicycle.

'I'll show you how to ride it,' he tells the younger children. 'You can take turns. No one touches the bike unless I'm around, all right?'

Aneesa is leaning against the bonnet of a car in the car park where the children play. It is an old blue estate that she has seen parked in the same spot for months and she does not feel she is doing it any harm.

The children have begun to arrive in twos and threes, filling up an otherwise empty Sunday afternoon. Some of them have bicycles, others come carrying a ball or a skateboard, while still others, she notices, arrive empty-handed, perhaps hoping to be included in a game with the others or are perhaps, like her, only here to watch.

A girl appears. She is dressed in jeans and a T-shirt and her hair is tied up in a high ponytail. Aneesa watches her approach a group of boys who seem to be organizing a football game. The little girl talks rapidly to them, gesturing with her hands, her eyes darting from one to the other. Moments later, the group disperses into two teams with a goalie at either end. The little girl, Aneesa is pleased to see, is on one of the teams and seems even more keen on playing than the others, running after the ball with wild determination and shrieking loudly whenever she gets it.

When the gap between their abilities seemed suddenly to have grown wider, Bassam would only play with Aneesa if their parents insisted on it or if there were no children his own age for him to play with. Aneesa remembers approaching him one day as he paced listlessly around the garden and telling him he had to play with her. I'll tell *baba* if you don't, Bassam. You know he'll be very angry with you.

Yet even when he had to be cajoled into it so that at the slightest mishap he would show irritation with her, playing with Bassam had made her immeasurably happy. She is not sure now whether it was because, as a child, she had admired her brother so much, or whether she is merely magnifying these incidents in her mind because he is no longer there. Does she romanticize their time together too much? What, Aneesa wonders, would my memories of our childhood have been like if Bassam had not disappeared? It is not poignancy she is searching for – although she is aware that her relationship with her brother is in danger of sinking into it with time – but a solid understanding of what it meant to have him in her life, a certainty that he had been there and that they had once existed, here, together.

Someone kicks the ball underneath the blue car. The

children all look in her direction. Aneesa watches as the little girl runs to fetch it. She looks up at Aneesa. Her cheeks are red and there are signs of perspiration on her forehead. The girl goes down on her knees and gets under the car. Aneesa is worried the girl might hurt herself. She squats down to make sure the child is all right.

'Did you find it?' Aneesa asks.

The girl's shoes make a scraping sound as she crawls out from underneath the car with the ball in her arms. They both stand up.

'I was worried the car might collapse on you,' Aneesa says with a grin.

The girl's clothes are covered with dust. She looks at Aneesa and flips back her ponytail with a shake of her head. She is not smiling.

'I'm all right,' she says before running back to her play-mates.

Aneesa nods and stands there for a few moments. The game has resumed and the children are no longer taking any notice of her. She turns away and heads for home.

What is Ramzi doing now, she wonders, or for that matter Samir? For a moment, she imagines them together, perhaps standing side by side on the Corniche, gazing at the Raouche Rock, or somewhere sitting in the outdoors eating ice cream cones, Samir urging Ramzi to be careful and not dirty his clothes, the sun shining behind them and making their features indistinct and mysterious.

Salah had once told her that as he got older he had felt a growing awareness of his past, an understanding of what had really been and his own role in it. It is not dwelling on what is gone, Salah explained, but a kind of reinterpretation of it so that you can finally be free of everything that once bound you and which will never come back again. Aneesa had tried to understand him but could not. The past is with me all the time, she told him, sometimes I think I am nothing else but who and what has come before me. How do you do it? But Salah had only smiled and run a hand over his hair, his fine, long fingers trembling a little.

Aneesa walks slowly until she reaches her block of flats. Clouds are beginning to form and the absence of sunlight seems to make the Sunday quiet more pronounced. She looks towards the water but can only see a thin sliver of it from this point, a far-off line of fluttering blue. She pulls the glass doors of the entrance open and summons the lift.

Waddad will have lunch ready once Aneesa gets upstairs. They will sit at the kitchen table and serve each other with obvious affection. They will eat and chat and once they are done, the clean dishes stacked dripping on the draining board to dry, the kitchen clock ticking behind them, Aneesa and Waddad will wander once again into their separate lives waiting for moments such as these to come their way again.

ENJOYED THIS BOOK? WHY NOT TRY OTHER GREAT HARPERCOLLINS TITLES – AT 10% OFF!

Buy great books direct from HarperCollins
at **10%** off recommended retail price.
FREE postage and packing in the UK.

☐ **Girl with a Pearl Earring** Tracy Chevalier 978-0-00-651320-9 **£6.99**

☐ **Falling Angels** Tracy Chevalier 978-0-00-718026-8 **£6.99**

☐ **The Virgin Blue** Tracy Chevalier 978-0-00-710827-5 **£6.99**

☐ **The Lady and the Unicorn** Tracy Chevalier 978-0-00-714090-9 **£6.99**

☐ **The Mapmaker's Opera** Béa Gonzalez 978-0-00-720779-4 **£6.99**

☐ **The Dead of Summer** Camilla Way 978-0-00-714344-3 **£6.99**

Total cost _____

10% discount _____

Final total _____

To purchase by Visa/Mastercard/Switch simply call
08707 871724 or fax on **08707 871725**

To pay by cheque, send a copy of this form with a cheque made payable to
'HarperCollins Publishers' to: Mail Order Dept. (Ref: BOB4),
HarperCollins Publishers, Westerhill Road, Bishopbriggs, G64 2QT,
making sure to include your full name, postal address and phone number.

From time to time HarperCollins may wish to use your personal data
to send you details of other HarperCollins publications and offers.
If you wish to receive information on other HarperCollins publications
and offers please tick this box ☐

Do not send cash or currency. Prices correct at time of press.
Prices and availability are subject to change without notice.
Delivery overseas and to Ireland incurs a £2 per book postage and packing charge.